DON'T MIND ME

Also by Brian Coughlan

Wattle & daub

Coughlan's stories wake us into the half-sleep of the familiar unknown, a sense of being late for an appointed fate. A writer of prodigious gifts, Coughlan combines irony with elements of surrealism to create a distinctively mordant and troubling, and, for all that, not unhumorous vision of the world.

—Colum McCann

In *Don't Mind Me*, Brian Coughlan's new story collection from Etruscan Press, narrators tell their straightforward, often calamitous, stories with great calm and control. But... there's always an uneasy feeling that something's coiled just beneath the surface. Like one of those fabric snakes compressed into a can labeled MIXED NUTS.

—Sara Pritchard, *Help Wanted: Female*

Darkly humorous and absurdist, *Don't Mind Me* entertains and enthralls throughout. Peculiar characters and situations populate these unexpected tales and with unique precision, Coughlan wittily reflects some of the disillusionment, disappointment and desperation of modern living.

—E. M. Reapy, *Skin* and *Red Dirt*

Brian Coughlan's second collection of short stories, *Don't Mind Me*, conjures surreal worlds and frequently hapless characters facing into a deluge of bizarre hurdles and catastrophes. By turns quirky and disquieting, with a dark, droll humor tempered with a humane perspective and insight throughout, these stories, intriguingly plotted and fiendishly envisaged, are consistently witty, surprising, and poignant in turn.

—Arnold Thomas Fanning, *Mind On Fire*

DON'T MIND ME

Brian Coughlan

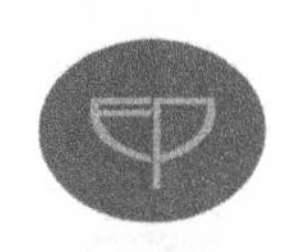

Etruscan Press

Etruscan Press
Wilkes University
84 West South Street
Wilkes-Barre, PA 18766
(570) 408-4546

Wilkes
University

www.etruscanpress.org

Published 2024 by Etruscan Press
Printed in the United States of America
Cover design by Logan Rock
Interior design and typesetting by Kari Bayait
The text of this book is set in Times.

First Edition

17 18 19 20 5 4 3 2 1

Library of Congress Cataloguing-in-Publication Data

Names: Coughlan, Brian, 1977- author.
Title: Don't mind me / Brian Coughlan.
Other titles: Don't mind me (Compilation) | Do not mind me
Description: First edition. | Wilkes-Barre, PA : Etruscan Press, 2024. |
Summary: "What begins as tragedy trips into farce, the realistic somehow turns mystical, and viewed through a prism of irony these delightfully off kilter stories offer surprising, often skewed and witfully unsettling impressions. Don't Mind Me is a collection that follows no rules and leaves no tracks"-- Provided by publisher.
Identifiers: LCCN 2023038962 | ISBN 9798985882483 (paperback ; acid-free paper) | ISBN 9798988198536 (ebook)
Subjects: LCGFT: Short stories.
Classification: LCC PR6103.O91 D66 2024 | DDC 823/.92--dc23/eng/20231002
LC record available at https://lccn.loc.gov/2023038962

Please turn to the back of this book for a list of the sustaining funders of Etruscan Press.

For Ciara, Jimmy, Seán & Áine

DON'T MIND ME

ACKNOWLEDGEMENTS

The Instrument
- appeared in *The Woven Tale Press*, Volume 7, (2020)

Motorcycle Man
- appeared in *Hearth & Coffin Literary Journal* (2021)

Deadbeats
- appeared in *The Honest Ulsterman* (2021)

A Beginners Guide to Taxidermy
- appeared in *Bear Creek Gazette* (2021)

A Nasty Fall
- appeared in *Anser Journal* (2021)

Pilloried
- appeared in *Littledeath Magazine* (2021)

A NASTY FALL

My fall was on a section of uneven concrete inside the stadium on a particularly bleak November day with a breeze that would cut the snout off your face. To think that I had strolled all the way there with the wrong throw-in time in my mind. I should have known that in winter with the early onset of darkness that the time might be fixed for earlier. It was only after the turnstile admitted me, a ticket stub clenched in one hand, a rolled-up match day programme in the other, I realized that the game was already well underway. I started hurrying towards the covered section of the dilapidated steel-grey stand; already visualizing that particular area I always try to find seating away from those obscuring poles and whether, due to my lateness, it would be still possible to get a half decent view of the match. Instead of looking where I was going and paying close attention to where my feet were landing, I caught the enormous febrile roar of the crowd—which team had scored?—and didn't notice just how uneven the surface of the ground was right in front of me.

In that patch of no-man's land, deserted apart from a couple of ragged stalls manned by hunched-over texting teens flogging chocolate bars and fizzy drinks, I stumbled, one foot kicking the other, and went down in a staggering slow-motion, suddenly picking up momentum the closer I came to the rough concrete with my hands extended. Pain instantly as sharp stones and pieces of grit embedded themselves in my palms to give me a poor man's stigmata. Not only that but my hip on the left side twisted oddly when I hit the ground, so hard that I ended up gasping in the dirt on one side like a fish on dry land flapping and straining uselessly—in the most appalling agony imaginable. The irony of it was that at this unusual angle, if even it was just for a few moments until help arrived, I had a very decent view of a long strip of the playing field and the young men clashing and fighting and straining to gain possession of the ball.

Strangely, the fall wrenched loose a memory seemingly out of nowhere; something I hadn't thought about in years and years. I'm standing motionless in my school playground, observing the collective insanity of schoolboys suddenly released from classrooms. A long-limbed boy tries to run past me. In doing so, he too trips, feet far behind and body lunging forward, and hits the ground hard; all that forward momentum meeting the solid asphalt playground. Like me all these years later, he examines his palms and picks out the tiny sharp stones embedded in soft yielding flesh. The major difference is that his boyhood mishap stalls him, only briefly, on a journey he's making to some other spot on the playground—he's running to burn off the excess energy of youth—as for me, forty years later, a cold November afternoon, the other side of the country—there was no getting up off the ground. I would have to stay down, and not only was I in physical pain, lying there, but my dignity, my self-respect, my inner strength were also injured in the fall.

Not that anybody had witnessed it. Everybody's attention was fixed on the match. I had gone down in an area where I was not visible to the crowd. The only ones who might spot me were those bored teenagers tending to the stalls, but they were too busy on their phones and, without customers bothering them, had retreated entirely from the outside world. I had to let out a roar. A desperate cry for help from the cold damp concrete. Eventually one of these kids heard me and ran over, stopping short of coming too close, as if I were contagious. Somehow intuiting the extent of my agony, he looked around wildly for somebody else to take charge before reluctantly approaching. He mumbled if I was ok? I emitted a series of involuntary agonized yelps and heard his runners scuffing off towards the stand. The next thing, a match day steward in a bright fluorescent jacket was kneeling beside me; a great looming face, stale breath, wincing empathetic expression, keeping me warm, talking to me gently, and reassuring me that everything would be fine.

It didn't take long for the ambulance to arrive because it was already present at the match. Its intended purpose was to take an injured player from the field of play, and instead it was transporting an injured spectator, who had not even made a decent job of spectating, to the nearest hospital. The worst part of it was that the game had to be stalled on my account because the ambulance had to drive onto the pitch and come around in a semicircle to get to where I was lying. Though thankfully the majority of people in the crowd could not see me, I could feel their frustration and annoyance as their entertainment was placed on hold for no obvious (and therefore satisfying) reason. Similarly the players on the field stood waiting with their hands on their hips or windmilling their arms to keep from getting cold. I'd managed to inconvenience the thousands of people in attendance by my carelessness and misfortune.

In the hospital various nurses who came and went gave me painkillers and left me behind a curtained-off triage area for many long and tedious hours. A tired-looking doctor briefly examined me. A monosyllabic radiologist X-rayed me. One short-fused and weary nurse confirmed that if I could control my bowel movements and support my own body weight there really was nothing that could be done. They said the fall had greatly aggravated a pre-existing condition, a ruptured disc and subsequent nerve damage, but an MRI scan would determine the full extent of the damage. Did I have a fully comprehensive medical insurance package that would cover all the costs associated? I did not. I had a very small, insignificant, badly wrapped package—the type of package nobody would willingly unwrap. I was prescribed more hefty painkillers and an anti-epileptic drug called gabapentin to treat possible nerve damage. To recover my power of movement would require intensive physiotherapy. They had done everything that could be reasonably expected of them: an examination, an X-ray, and a prescription for drugs to dull the pain. The rest was up to me.

In the weeks that followed I was inundated with people telling me what had worked for them. Everybody, from my dentist to my barber to my work colleagues, offered their advice on what I should do to get myself 'fixed-up'. It must have been my permanently stooped shuffling gait or constant grimacing every time I tried to sit down or stand up that emboldened them to lecture me on what had worked for them. Things were just as bad at home. The evening I was discharged, my gratingly sympathetic wife (more pillows, less pillows, more painkillers, more water, something to eat, need a hand going to the toilet) kept asking aloud how something like this could have happened to a relatively young man? What could she do to make it better? There had to be something. What could she do to take away the constant pain? Nothing. Nothing at all.

The thing I found most difficult after the fall was putting on my socks and shoes. A task I'd always performed by bringing one foot after the other to knee height and guiding the sock over the toes, before dropping down to either knee and tying the shoelace quickly and efficiently without having to give any kind of consideration, was no longer feasible. My lower back and hip were locked and stiffened each morning with a dull pain originating on my left side and running down along the hip and through the buttock all down my leg and around the ankle right to the very furthest tip of my big toe. I now had to hoist each leg in turn up onto the kitchen table and cast off, using my sock in the manner of a fly-fisherman hoping to snag a big toe.

Yoga was suggested by somebody. I tried using an online yoga video tailored specifically, it said, for back pain sufferers. One of the exercises was to put a rolled-up beach towel over the foot while lying on one's back to bring the leg upwards and stretch out the foot against the rolled-up towel, with either end of the towel held right and left. A few minutes after performing this manoeuvre I was visited once again by pain. Off the scale pain. Every nerve of the left leg spasticating the muscle into rigidity. The spasm and the jerk of nerves rippled their way right through the center of my being to leave me in a state of fully hysterical anguish; then wailing and thrashing around the house in search of painkillers, I fought my way to the shower and under ice-cold water screamed and bellowed, as excruciating spasms wrenched my muscles into tight screaming bundles and then delivered a strange numbness throughout my left leg.

Sucking on a large syringe of morphine I assured the A&E nurse with complete seriousness that there was no possible way childbirth could be more painful than what I was experiencing. Another examination confirmed that I could support my own body weight and I was not incontinent, ergo there was absolutely nothing they could do. Any surgery in that particular part of the anatomy would be complicated. The only thing for it was to have an MRI scan to confirm what they already suspected, which was that discs had ruptured and consequently all the nerves in the area were being pinched and aggravated with every movement of my body.

Then came the chiropractors, faith healers, back-cracking specialists, bone setters, osteopaths—a raggedy crew of manipulators and quacks I encountered on my limping pilgrimage towards living with constant pain and discomfort. None of their treatments did anything to improve my condition—if anything they deepened my sense of desperation, my willingness to try anything. Acupuncture is the latest stop on this dismal journey. My first appointment started with Dr Xi filling out a sheet of paper with his tiny snub-nosed pencil. The treatment room was a sitting room in a domestic dwelling converted to a surgery office by flimsy means. He had me walk around and repeatedly sit down and stand up in the cramped and windowless space. He examined my boxer-short-wearing-self with a hand pressed to his chin. He would need to figure out what the problem was. I had pain in my lower back but where did it really originate from? That was the seemingly philosophical question he was posing to himself. Having stuck a few needles in me and placed a blanket over my shoulder I was left lying on a bed in the tiny room with the curtains pulled and an incense stick burning.

On the mantlepiece of his treatment room above an unused fireplace, painted on a black matt background, on what appeared to be a thin piece of wood, was a figure that I struggled to make sense of. It was difficult to establish what the picture consisted of until I began to interpret an image: a garland of cherry blossoms around the central figure of a woman in a long flowing dress of the kind concealing a whalebone corset and legs in white tights. Head bowed over to one side. Her expression inscrutable but endlessly mysterious. It drew my attention, offered no hint of explanation or meaning, simply distracted the patient from the tedium of lying there in a converted sitting room, the low lighting, the hum of traffic at the intersection outside.

Before I find an answer to the riddle of the picture, he's back and removing the needles. When asked if my pain has receded I'm forced to lie to him. And on two further visits I tell him how effective his treatment is proving when in fact I'm only grasping at straws (or is it needles?), hoping for a miracle to relieve the almost constant pain. He has me stand up and sit down. He has me roll around. He has me touch my toes. Each time I perform these tasks he rewards me with 'very good' and a series of grunting noises as he scribbles on the piece of paper that contains all of my details and a crude outline drawing of the human body.

The peculiar childhood memory replayed itself from that same angle I had as I lay on the ground, as the match continued with sheer indifference to my suffering, as the match day steward tucked his puffy fluorescent jacket around me to keep me warm, as the crowd roared its approval at some feat of skill or daring from one of those players. I was carried back to that moment in the schoolyard, alone among a horde of screaming animals, surveying a scene that was happening right there in front of me but without my participation. Unable to find my way in I wandered around the outside and simply observed what was happening, all the arguments, all the pushing and shoving, all the screaming and name-calling, and I focused on that skinny, long-legged boy rushing full pelt towards me, and in that split-second I decided, or rather something decided on my behalf, to become a participant in what was happening out there—stick out your foot, trip him!

Still in considerable discomfort, I phone to schedule another appointment to see the acupuncturist. There are some openings in his calendar. His secretary rhymes them out and tells me in her querulous voice that it's up to me which one of them I want. I don't believe her: it's entirely not up to me. We unwittingly do and say what has been prescribed for us. We never have a choice in the matter, just the vaguely comforting illusion that we do. It wasn't up to me that I fell and incapacitated myself. It wasn't me that tripped the boy. At least that's the conclusion I've embraced while lying here on the floor of my living room, staring at the ceiling, slowly extending each leg in turn as part of an exercise regime in futility.

I close my eyes and return again and again to that still lucid playground scene with the long-limbed boy whipping around, once he had regained his footing, to see who or what had tripped him. Did he realize that I was the one responsible for his fall? Did he know it was my outstretched foot? I imagine a sneer plastered across my face and a provocative ready to fight stance, head cocked to one side. I expected to see a look of fury and outrage on his, but instead he glowered with contempt, picked the stones out of his palms, and without another moment's hesitation dived right back into the fray, merging with the others into one screaming entity, scruffy headed, all arms and legs, runny noses, wild eyes, full blown feral.

The acupuncturist's secretary wants to know if I'm still on the line. She mis-spoke a moment ago. Tuesday, Wednesday, and Thursday are completely out of the question, all she has left is a Friday morning slot.

Will that do?

KEYS CUT WHILE YOU WAIT

She was now exactly twenty-three minutes late. Unwisely, he had inhaled two generous tumblers of whiskey, thinking it would make him more at ease, more comfortable in his own skin, dramatically increase his suaveness. Instead the alcohol activated a repellent side to his personality, a side that clung always to the most pessimistic brand of lifebuoy bobbing in an open sea of fathomless misery. This side was winning him over to the idea that 'she' did not actually exist in reality, that he had made a date with an algorithm, or worse, some time-wasting fraud who took a perverse pleasure in doing this kind of thing to lonely singletons. Wasn't it entirely possible that at this very moment he was being filmed by a team of undercover pranksters and live streamed on some newly created social media site dedicated to the exposure and ridicule of desperately lonely losers?

Not being much of a drinker under normal circumstances (was it just two or was it three whiskies?) the alcohol had taken immediate effect. He could feel his thoughts slipping around in the muck and a vaguely uncomfortable buzz of background anxiety chewing away at already frayed nerves. Observing every jilted movement of the big hand on his expensive recently purchased wristwatch to which he was biometrically twinned (pulse racing, heart hammering, bowels chiming) he wondered at what point to admit that he had been stood-up and quietly leave the restaurant with his dignity hanging down somewhere between his legs.

A full thirty minutes late seemed generous. He imagined being late for a first date or even a job interview, and if he was half an hour late the chances are he'd have given up even trying and slowed down to a stroll, throwing his hands in the air. Just another seven minutes or thereabouts of excruciating shame and embarrassment to be endured until he could end this dreadfully humiliating farce.

The pitying waiter, passing at irregular intervals, would pause to ask if he was ready to order something, or was he going to leave it another while? Not that he was trying to make a holy show of him or anything like that. In fact, quite the opposite, the waiter spoke so discreetly under his breath, one hand covering his mouth, and even winked with a gentle tilt of the head, as if to say: I feel your pain, man. Ronnie ignored him. Buried his head in the menu again. Read the same descriptions through again. Continued to ponder over the impenetrable names of the pretentious-sounding dishes. Much of the menu had been foraged in the nearest woodland earlier that same day; the water pumped from a sustainable local aquifer; the napkins made from organic yak urine; the meat sourced from corn-fed and perfectly happy to be slaughtered pigs, sheep, and cattle. Everything else had been grown on a rooftop garden using ethically sourced bird shit as fertilizer and recycled urine for no apparent reason other than to recycle the urine. The menu informed him of all this in the shrillest tone imaginable.

The poor man had himself driven demented, convinced beyond all reasonable doubt that the people at nearby tables were secretly stealing glances in his direction. Guarding their smiles with menus large enough to act as shields, they were passing comment on his pinkish perspiring head and fogged-up designer glasses. It really didn't look like his date was going to make an appearance, did it? Because there was no reason why she shouldn't have sent him a message through the dating app. Especially if she was simply running a little late for some perfectly understandable reason: like a road accident or a death in the family. Unless of course she had changed her mind about the whole thing and was planning to ghost him, in which case he should immediately gather up the remnants of his self-respect, pay the waiter for his drinks, and slither into the night.

Unless 'she' was not real. Back to this again! Unless he had made a date with an algorithm that knew from his preferences and likes exactly what to say to him. The over and back of messages. That perceived 'sense of humor'. It could have all been faked so very easily. The more he obsessed the more he felt light-headed, sick to the pit of his stomach. Where could the cameras be hidden? Worse, what if someone that knew him walked in the door or, worse again, was already here, lurking in the candlelight?

Why was he even here? Why? It was absolutely pathetic. All dressed-up in his new sports jacket, shirt open to reveal tightly clipped chest hair, nasal hair trimmed perfectly, the few tufts on the top of his head fluffed and repositioned with styling foam. All of his preparation and giddiness replaced by the crushing embarrassment of having been stood up. This was exactly why he'd never bothered to try online dating before—it was all a load of fake bullshit and peopled with timewasters!

He had far better things to do than sit here on a Thursday night staring into the abyss and drinking. Oh fuck! He'd just turned over the menu to the drinks side for the first time all evening—every single one of the whiskies were incredibly expensive. The cheapest was 45 euro a shot. Was he even drinking the cheapest one? No wonder the waiter was winking at him. He'd been played like a cheap mandolin. The gods were really having some fun with him this evening, lounging around in their loin cloths, and giving each other high-fives.

He picked up his mobile phone and snarled at the butter-wouldn't-melt profile picture before draining the last dregs of a whiskey that he had no memory of having ordered. He had to get a grip of himself. Was this his second or third? Lilting music from some Tahitian dreamscape emanating from speakers concealed by the lush jungle flora failed to soothe his annoyance. At least another minute had passed. That was something to be thankful for. But really his mind was working on the possibility of leaving without paying the bill. There had to be a way. There had to be some means of slipping away into the night and putting this whole sorry business behind him, because that was what he intended to do, pretend it never happened. Except that Ronnie would never have the balls to slip out without paying, and he knew it. It would plague him, it would eat away at him—he wasn't entirely sure if it meant he had integrity, but it was at least some part of the delusion.

The next moment, she was right there in front of him, clutching a clutch bag.

"Terry?"

He needed a moment to compose himself, to recover from the shock of her actual physical presence, until it dawned on him just how rudely he was behaving (he should pull back her chair for her to sit down) and so he clambered into the standing pose of a long-armed mountain gorilla. So rapid and ungainly was his great leap up the evolutionary furniture that a jug filled with aquifer water was toppled and hit the tiled floor with a deafening metallic gong. Ice, water, and a couple of lemon slices flowed freely down the middle of the floor through flooded forests, vast grasslands, and a wide delta before ending their epic journey at the base of an accent wall studded with eye-gouging knick-knacks.

The only problem was that his name was not Terry. Also there was no avoiding the fact that she did not look anything like the person in the profile picture. *Say something you great ape*, thought Ronnie, but truly nothing at all came to mind. From behind a screen of unwanted intoxication that had rendered his tongue almost entirely inflexible, he tried to form some suitable response; this woman was quite stunning now that he allowed himself the time to study her face and note her elegant features. He could tell that she had an equally beautiful personality because she had not yet dismissed him as a possible date for the evening, despite his imbecilic bearing, mouth wide open, and nothing even remotely intelligible coming out.

Presently a towering figure approached their table to introduce himself as Terry and very nearly ripped Ronnie's hand clean-off his arm during their hurried handshake. The three of them stared over and back for ages. Terry just standing there, knees locked out, his hands in his pockets, clenching and unclenching his fists, which is why his pockets continued to bulge and then deflate as his legs continuously swayed in and out.

"...think there's been a bit of a..."

"You're waiting for...?"

"...Kate."

"Terry."

Bingo! That was *her* name. Ronnie sat down again and pretended to find it all highly amusing, grinning so hard and so inauthentically that it actually made his face ache. It was ratcheting up very nicely. Kate and Terry vanished. Or at least reconvened to a table two meters away. Behind a large potted plant, thankfully. If there was a hole he could have climbed into. Actually he was already in the hole. Now was the time to get out of the hole by leaving money on the table and running for the door. But first things first: he desperately needed to use the bathroom, that was his immediate priority, and then to get out of this place for good. He asked for the cheque by making a squiggle in the air as he stumbled towards the toilets.

Was he possibly a little bit drunk or had the other diners deliberately left bags and coats in the walkway between the tables?

In the men's room, once he had concluded his business, he noticed a small window above the urinals. Escape route? No, it was locked and bolted securely. Sheepishly he returned to the pine scented waterfall, surveyed his options, and noticed an air handling unit running all along the ceiling. He had a truly mad thought. If he stood up on the sink, caught hold of the air ducting grille (the bolts were rusted to a fine dust) and yanked off the grille, could he then climb inside? Was it possible? He imagined hauling himself inside the tight metallic chamber to begin a burrowing, crawling, journey, with the penetrating light from his phone guiding him forward, brushing aside his near future like a cobweb: that frozen pizza, those endless bottles of bland beer, and flicking hurriedly from station to station on his enormously curving high-definition screen.

The alcohol in his system gave him the impetus to try and catch hold of the air handling unit—just for the hell of it. It was a silly thing to do, especially since he was wearing leather soled shoes. Especially since he was intoxicated. Especially since he was in a highly emotional state. On initial contact with the ceramic, his shoes lost all possible grip. He came down hard, his chin catching the edge of the sink as an uppercut, that left him sprawled and unconscious on the tiled bathroom floor. He was discovered ten minutes later by a man dying for a piss, who went to the trouble of alerting the waiter, who went to the trouble of alerting the manager, who insisted that an ambulance be called despite Ronnie's protests.

Too ashamed and embarrassed to stay on the ground and remembering that his coat was still hanging from the coat stand, the stricken man rose up on unsteady legs and faltered back into the restaurant with the aid of the waiter. His date for the evening had just arrived and was seating herself at their table. A full hour late for their first date. Imagine. It really and truly beggared belief. Seeing a visibly distressed man stumbling towards her the woman rose and knocked a full jug of water onto the tiled floor where it produced a deafening gong, sending ice and lemon slices flowing freely down the middle of the floor, in rivulets that joined and parted at intervals before pooling in a vaguely heart-shaped puddle.

The poor thing was so dishevelled: the knee of his trouser leg was torn, he appeared to have a large bruise above one eye, and the little tuft of hair on his head combined with his mournful expression put her in mind of a toddler, a confused two-year-old wandering around in a dirty nappy.

"You really did everything you could, didn't you!" she said, giving Ronnie a wide heart-warming smile. She informed him that his deliberate attempt to confuse the time of their date was really cute and attractive, when looked at from a certain angle. A deliberate attempt at self-sabotage. She then went on to admonish him, that he shouldn't sell himself short like that; that everyone had something to offer. Didn't he agree? Well? Hello in there!

Ronnie held back tears of self-pity and rage, but only just.

Her smile broadened, her lips parted, and she stuck out her tongue at him. Just for an instant. Just to alert him to the person behind the mask. The over-familiarity of her manner had completely unnerved Ronnie. He felt somehow that they were previously acquainted though he had no idea in what context—or at least *she* felt acquainted with *him*. But what was the context? Until he knew that much...

"Will you please, sit down, like a good man" said the stranger.

They picked up a menu each and Ronnie seized the opportunity to hide behind the laminated plastic. Heart thumping, he hoped that the thin material would somehow stop the transmission of his thoughts into her head, and he waited uncertainly for her to say something else. He was so frightened he couldn't decide what to order off the menu, never mind start a meaningful conversation with a bona fide person. If he could get to his phone, without her noticing, at least he could try and recover her name. To address her, not as some stranger from the street who wanted to mess with his mind, but as a genuine presence would surely help him recover his poise. If he could get to his phone and retrace his steps in terms of their flirtation through the dating app, maybe then he would remember who he was pretending to be, because at present he was completely lost, incapable of striking a pose, or even making an attempt at being himself.

"Caroline," she murmured from the other side of the menu.

Ronnie stopped nervously fingering his phone and made a supreme effort to pull himself together, once and for all. His behaviour all evening had been shockingly infantile. There really was no other word for it. Infantile. The great problem was that he didn't understand how other people worked. How their minds worked. No, a step back, he didn't understand how his own mind worked. If he couldn't understand his own mind then how could he present himself to the world as a legitimate person? It was absurd to think that producing inarticulate babble and hoping that that babble would be accepted by another entity as proof of legitimacy would be enough to get him out of the prison inside his skull, even for one evening. It was an absurd game, the rules of which had never been adequately explained to him, and yet everyone else knew them off by heart.

"Are we going to sit here in silence all evening?" asked Caroline.

Taking the hint, Ronnie lowered his laminated plastic shield, to ask Caroline if she'd had far to come. All subsequent questions also contained her name so that he should not forget it again.

The rest of the evening proceeded along the usual lines.

When it was time to leave, a thoroughly worn-out Ronnie allowed himself to be carried up the stairs and strapped into the back of a waiting car-seat. On the ride home he desperately tried to keep his eyes open but the sensation of the car's movement through the dark streets and warm air rushing into his face made it impossible to hold out. He fell into a deep dreamless sleep and even when she changed him out of his clothes into pyjamas that had been warming on a radiator—he still did not so much as bat an eyelid. Even when he was lifted roughly onto a shoulder, with his head lolling every which way, and clumsily fumbled in the act of putting him down for the night—nothing. Not so much as a stir out of him. Out cold.

THE INSTRUMENT

The two outer clasps undone, it crawled out and sniffed nervously around our feet. Then, having produced a small stool, the instrument tried to scuttle back inside its protective case. A repeatedly stamping high-heeled boot barred it from doing so. The woman selling the instrument pointedly refused to open the two inner clasps: it would remain muzzled while we bargained. For an indeterminate amount of time, all three of us, the seller, me, and my father, stared in mute fascination at its scratchy frightened movements around her living room floor. The shiny leather straps and opalescent effect of the bodywork made a deeply unpleasant first impression. There was that cold gut feeling of potential exposure to the unknown. I was a boy who liked to go unnoticed. This instrument would require a commitment, an undertaking, an approach towards something above and beyond me. It would create expectations because this untamed, unwieldy *thing* was intended for me—it would be mine to look after, and to one day, master.

Our attempted wrangle was from a woman in a long flowery skirt, long droopy earrings, long ringlet-laden hair, and a long humourless face, who had reached the end of her tether as far as this curious item was concerned. *Nerves must have been at her* was how she was later described by my father, to anyone who would listen. She was chain smoking cigarettes, all brown stubby fingers belonging to a blue-veined, shaking hand. The instrument's asking price was next to nothing. Her desire was to part ways with it on favourable terms. My father wouldn't even give her the pittance she was asking for. He shook his head and walked away. This had been a complete waste of his time. Her response was to light another cigarette and shrug her shoulders. More like a waste of *her* time, actually. I breathed a huge sigh of relief. No deal was likely to happen while they were both so angry by all the time that had been wasted.

Of course, I was too young then to understand that this wordless terse struggle was all just part of the bargaining dance. All part of the preordained moves of undervaluing and running into the ground the item that you secretly desire. And on her part the take-it or leave-it shrug of shoulders about a thing you desperately want to get rid of. I did not know the steps yet was dragged, kicking and screaming, out onto the dancefloor, when my father told me to give it a try on for size, at the very least. To see if I liked the feel of it. As if my liking the instrument had anything to do with it. As if liking it made a blind bit of difference to a man blinded with grand notions, a man who had already decided that his son would gain control of this instrument for the greater glory of our family name.

To appease him, the seller reluctantly strapped me into it, and the leather fastenings were pulled taut across my back, the tightening of each one with the ache of leather, pushing the air out of my lungs in a protracted wheeze. Across both shoulders and over the back of my right hand every strap was tightened and strained with the full force of an angry and humiliated stranger. It was like an orthopaedic attachment by the time she'd fully secured me. My lanky frame sagged forward, under its astonishing weight, as I struggled for breath.

"Play something!" said my father.

Never having touched one before, I didn't know where to start, I mean there were keys on one side and buttons on the other. So many keys and so many buttons. There was too much choice. He tried to help by shoving my elbow. Nothing happened. Father was dubious and so the poor woman was forced to undo the inner clasps. Then he shoved my elbow again so that I pressed down on one white key and, keeping it depressed the entire time, opened out the instrument like a peacock's tail and then pulled it all back inwards again in one long continuous groaning dirge of ear-splitting honk. My father's face decompressed into a singular rictus; the woman began to dry retch until she developed a self-sustaining coughing fit that turned her face puce; and, as for me, I caught a bout of painfully elaborate hiccups that lasted over an hour.

It was in the first desperate honk of the instrument that I knew with absolute conviction I would never produce a sound of any beauty with it. I knew from that very first moment of contact that there would no love between us. The instrument hated my adolescent guts. I wanted to take it off my shoulders, but the adults were arguing over the price. My hand was stuck in a place where the smaller buttons pricked me as the edges of the bellows jostled me in the ribs and as my back began to ache from the weight of the thing. When their eyes were averted I punched the body of the instrument and growled at it, like a dog. In retaliation it closed itself on my finger, trapping it painfully among the foldings. It was voicing its displeasure at being squeezed, poked, and man-handled by an acne covered teen with not so much as a whiff of under arm musicality.

Father wouldn't listen to my protests. Instead he took the trouble to explain to me that I would one day be able to bring a party to life by the mellifluous sound of this most treasured, most revered of instruments. I couldn't share in his vision for my future: the imagined foot tapping, the fingers leaping up and down, the smile of satisfaction on faces as the listeners clapped their hands and stomped their feet in time to the sweet, sweet, music. I just couldn't see it. I couldn't share his vision of me and this instrument combined into one entity acting as the centre of attention for delirious partygoers in some imagined shindig. In any case, my protests were in vain because they came *after* the instrument had been purchased. I could only use them, after the fact, as evidence for my prospective failure. They were a down-payment on his eventual disappointment.

The seller refused to go any lower on the price. Her voice quavered. "Get the boy out of it," she said, staring at me without compassion. Father shook his head ruefully and walked away. He was pretending to be angry and done with the whole affair. He shouted over his shoulder for me to get back into the van. At which point she called him back. I was the only one surprised when she did. What a blessed relief it was to leave that stuffy front room filled with porcelain figurines, strange plastic covered dolls, and mangy teddy bears that I was warned repeatedly not to touch. No, she wouldn't take a personal cheque. It had to be cash in hand. It had to be a series of rolled-up dirty notes from an unusual side pocket, handed to her with a barely concealed contempt.

I had to wear it strapped to my chest all the way back in the van; there wasn't time to take it off. We were in a hurry. We were always in a hurry. Imagine her wanting more money for the box it came in. He'd make one from plywood and salvaged door hinges. On the journey home through the falling darkness, it was made clear to me by his disembodied voice that the instrument was a serious investment in my future and that any resistance to his vision was futile. All I had to do now was forget about the petty distractions that would otherwise cloud the mind of an eleven-year-old boy, especially the kind of pretend wrestling that he forbade me from watching on our tiny black and white television.

Right from the off, our relationship was fraught. I could never trust that the key I pressed would produce the sound I expected because the instrument was forever changing its mind about its keys. In practise, this meant that I was forced to squeeze and wrestle with both hands as it strained beneath me to rid itself of my long prodding fingers. With enough violence shown, an understanding could be arrived at where some kind of raggedy halting tune emerged, but this would instantly vanish once another person entered the room. Then the instrument would revolt and force my fingers to hit all the wrong keys, or rather the right keys from before, but not now, not when there was another person in attendance.

Lessons were required. In the middle of our quaint little town was a general-purpose hall abutting a coal depot. The inside of the hall was damp and mouldy. The floor was of old wooden boards that threw-up dust at the slightest provocation. By that I mean any movement no matter how small caused a plume of thick dust to rise and catch in the back of the throat. This was the place where I would learn the basics of instrument playing. I was abandoned at the hall on Wednesdays, a day I grew to dread every week. At the mercy of dust and slanting shards of light through cobwebbed windows, I was forced to sit in a ring of other instrument players as the teacher moved from one student to the next.

Giving each of us a five-minute time slot she listened closely and provided her wise words of instruction, but how she could have heard a single note is beyond me because each and every one of the instrument players in that cramped hall were playing at one and the same time. Can you imagine a small room in a tiny hall, in a derelict part of town, next to a coal yard, near a fair-green, over-looking a car dealership, next to a bakery, through a worn wrought iron gate and the sound of twenty instruments honking out twenty different tunes, all out of sync, and with the furious moving fingers and huge piercing bellow sounds of beginners with any instrument but especially—especially the instrument allotted to each of us, the loudest of all the instruments?

Every night I was reminded by a snide remark from a sister or eyes above the newspaper to go and practise my playing in the kitchen. There was no point in fighting it. All I could do was slump out of the room with downcast eyes and drooping shoulders. Good money had been spent on the instrument and on lessons and that there was no earthly way I was going to get out of playing it. Did I voice my reluctance? I am sure that I did—but at the same time let me explain that I was not the kind of child to throw a tantrum. I was the kind of child who did as he was told and did not question the greater reason why.

The practising went up several notches in our linoleum and pine kitchen until a family member entered the room for food or water or simply to go from one part of the house to another. As soon as they entered the room I would stop playing and stare at them. The mastery of this complex and moody instrument could not happen with someone watching, or worse listening, to what I was doing. It must have been my pretend dedication and serious demeanour that convinced my family I would become proficient at playing the instrument. In reality I was self-flagellating with the same song *Kelly the Boy from Killane* that I massacred time and time again in a halting, error strewn manner, until the inner clasps fastened themselves and the whole apparatus clamped shut with a sudden sullen finality.

One morning I was woken up from an appalling nightmare by my father. He was dressed in a suit and tie. It was as if he was going to a wedding. I was forced into my Sunday best. We travelled in silence. My stomach was ready to uncoil like a snake with nervous anticipation. I had been warned this day would come, but I had had no idea what lay ahead of me. It wasn't until we got to the school, until we were sitting in a classroom with other parents and their children, the instruments scrapping like dogs, it was only then that the sheer leaping horror of having to play my one pitiful tune for these assembled people began to dawn. I had never even played for my own family and now I was here to play for these strangers. How was this supposed to be achieved. I can't imagine how it was ever decreed to be feasible.

The worst part was the waiting to be called up to play. The sheer dawning realization that you will be expected to get up and walk to the centre of the room with your instrument to play in front of everyone. Each player seemed nervous as they came to the seat but then the sweetest of music flowed from their instrument with the slightest effort required and we could all relax and enjoy it. It just happened as easily as breathing in and out. A smile on the lips and a foot tapping along with the nods of appreciation in the audience. And then the realization that I was not fit to tie the shoelaces of these people. I was disgracefully short of the required standard to be in the same room and each one better than the last. Virtuoso performances. Sweet music played the way it ought to be—with passion and flair by boys and girls who love what they are doing.

Hiding away inside the body of that boy was the mighty shaking soul of a coward. A boy quaking in his boots. A boy who would rather be anywhere else in the world. And just why had he been born anyway if this was the end result? The thought of running away, while certainly tempting was simply farcical as was saying to his father *I really don't want to do this*. They were here now, the instrument was at his feet, it was just a case of getting on with it. The moment of his name being called. The self-conscious walk across the room with head bowed. Seated and ready to go. Safety catches removed from the top and yet...

From my father's perspective: all the money spent on those expensive lessons, surely to Christ he can play something. It's been six months. Get up there and show these people what you're made of. Stop slouching. Why does he have to slouch! Be confident. Ok. Come on now. Why isn't he playing something? Play. Jesus Christ, play something. Play. Play something. Oh Christ, please! Play something. Just make a start. If he only pressed one button. Play something. Oh Lord, please, I'm begging you—Sweet Jesus please help my son. I promise I'll... Oh no, Oh Jesus Christ please, help him play something. That's it! Good man. Yes, that's it. He's off. Thank Christ. Thank You, Thank You, Thank You! Here we go; yes, he's off. He's playing something and I don't care how bad it is.

As I pressed the keys and opened and closed the bellows, the atmosphere in the room began to change, to assume a taut breathless mugginess. Nobody could draw a breath. The room was suddenly boiling, overwhelmingly crowded with bodies and full of restive children needing to be shushed by anxious parents. Ungainly music began to seep from the instrument like a poisonous gas. There was no way of escaping. The doors and windows were closed. The listeners began to claw at their neck ties, men grew faint, women braced themselves, children cried out in fear. The instrument had decided, in its infinite wisdom, to do something entirely other than the tune I was trying to play. It had decided to evoke the memory of the bedraggled woman who had sold it to my father and in the style of an interminable dirge dragging itself bloodied and beaten to a whimpering collapse.

How my performance ended is still a mystery. It was surely an out of body type experience, but the relief of finishing and that polite applause gave way quickly to the sudden burn of shame. Father refused to make eye contact and muttered at me to run for the van when all the doors and windows in the classroom were thrown open to let in some badly needed air. I stumbled outside, undoing the straps, bursting with relief, and knowing that the spell was broken, the vision obscured, my childhood once again restored. The instrument stayed with us for a couple of months following the competition and remained happily entombed in its plywood coffin until some poor wretch answered the advertisement in the local paper and took it off our hands.

These days its memory is evoked when I am called upon to speak in public, to raise my voice, to stand up tall and speak my mind to a group of people, especially strangers; to make my presence felt, as I am now about to, any moment now, on this very sad occasion. As always I feel the straps tighten around my chest and my breath shorten and the phantom weight pulls me forward so that I assume the curiously hideous shape of the man before you this evening, waiting for his name to be called, to walk up to the lectern and to deliver the eulogy, with this awful gaping expectation from the mourners in front of me and behind me, and on my left side and on my right side, and all of them expecting me to render his life into my own.

LADDER

A long metallic kind of ladder. Telescopic. It can be extended out to twice its normal length by undoing side clasps. It's the kind of ladder that sways and slightly buckles the higher up it you go. You climb by grabbing hold of the rungs and scooting upwards—despite the fact that it's resting up against nothing. You are climbing up into space. The ladder has been adjusted by two pieces of folded-up cardboard under the feet, to account for the uneven nature of the concrete ground; then you start to climb, slowly and methodically. There is no need to rush and to do so might cause the ladder to tip over one way or the other. It's highly unlikely to fall away either side of you because of the cardboard under the feet. It could tip backwards so that you are crushed by it falling on top of you, or it could pitch forward in which case you will face plant into the ground and most likely crush your fingers in the process. Which is why you take your time and climb vertically straight up. Nice and easy. One step at a time. Get into the rhythm of it. Climbing higher and higher. At some point you may need to come back down, but that's not even worth thinking about. Just keep climbing. The trick is to not look up or down. If you look down then you will lose your balance and fall. If you look up you will see nothing but the sky and possibly clouds and you'll falter. Keep climbing the ladder. Put one hand over the other and pull upwards as one foot rises a rung at a time and is joined by its brother. The ladder was borrowed from your wife's grandmother. You told her it was to clean the gutters of all the gunk that accumulates in gutters over time, but the truth is that you wanted to climb the ladder straight up into the sky, and you just knew that if you asked her for the ladder and explained what you really wanted it for, she would have had a long list of questions, and more questions on top of the answers, and more questions again, until both you and her would end up baffled and frustrated by the evasiveness of your responses. To be truthful about it you haven't got a clue why this was so important in the first place. You just got it into your head that you needed to climb a ladder, and nothing would do you but to climb it.

When you get to the top rung, it's going to be interesting because at that point you won't be able to go any further unless you pull the bottom half of the ladder up after you, say by using a piece of rope tied to the top rung of the bottom half of the ladder and the other end looped around your wrist. Except you didn't think of it until you'd already started climbing. It was too late then to go looking for a piece of rope long enough (especially when you know that you don't have a length of rope long enough) so you had to keep going and deal with the problem as you come to it, and that's what you plan to do—just keep climbing up and see what happens. The best part of it is that you are completely alone, and there isn't anyone around to watch what you are doing because you took the time to wait for everyone to leave for work and school and the creche. You took the time and then when everyone was gone—out came the ladder and up you started—slowly of course, to begin with because of your sore knees but then slightly faster once you got into the rhythm of it. A long telescopic ladder. You are climbing up at a steady pace into what is a terribly grey sky—perfect climbing conditions—and the rain lashing straight down and the wind blowing from every direction and leaves falling onto the rungs along with the rain. Perfect, perfect conditions to climb a ladder on a Tuesday morning, while the rest of the world is busy making money or keeping itself occupied by other means. It's not as if climbing upwards is something to be frowned upon, but it may require you to stand on a few hands of the ones who are coming after you. That's bullshit right there. That's the first bum note. This isn't about anybody else—this is about climbing a ladder and nothing more than that. You don't care who follows you up the ladder or who went before you up the ladder. All of that is completely irrelevant to the here and now. Just one rung at a time. Like you said earlier, once you get to the top things will get interesting, until then just stick with the program, nice and easy does it, no sudden movements, or useful thoughts to improve the process—just keep doing what you know and are most comfortable with—and that's climbing up this ladder at a nice and steady pace.

Wait. There's someone at home in the house across the street. Smoking a cigarette. In a pink dressing gown. That's ruined it. That's taken the wind out of your sails. It's not the same anymore. Now she has started to film you with her mobile phone. Why do people feel entitled to do that? Is it because she's afraid that nobody will believe her if she tells them and doesn't have evidence to support her claims? Is that it? The answer is irrelevant. The question is beside the point. You start to come down one rung at a time, and it's fine until you start to think about the fact that somebody is filming you coming down the ladder, so you start to wobble, you start to buck, you start to shake. It's because you're such a people-pleaser and you know damn well that if you fall off the ladder or if the ladder tips over in either direction it will make her video even more viral, even more viewable. You can't help it. It's something in you that wants so desperately for other people to accept you for who you are without condescending or flattering their ego. And there lies the problem, and beside it, there you lie, struggling to come to terms with another disappointment, struggling to regain the use of your arms and legs. You thought you heard a crack. You thought you heard a bone crack or a ligament or a tendon. The main thing is that she captured it all on her phone. That's the important part. What happened might never have happened without a recording of the event. When it gets dark you should be able to crawl back inside the house. The ladder is fine where it is: sticking out at an acute angle from the middle of the hedge. From a hedge that really needs trimming. Anyway, that's another day's work. Just stay still, keep calm, and wait for the return of your wife from work; you are only guaranteed her sympathy if she finds you in the hedge. Were you to climb out of your own accord she would only start asking you questions—stay where you are. A feeble bleat when she steps out of her car will suffice. I know it hurts but what can you do? Exactly. Take full advantage of the situation.

DON'T MIND ME

That expensive Persian rug in the vestibule is not for treading on. The elegant three-legged telescope carefully positioned on the upstairs landing is not for looking through. The immaculate living room couch, still covered in a plastic film, is not to be disturbed by your looming derriere. Instead, think of the modern-day B&B with all of its petty unwritten rules as a place to store yourself, or more accurately your physical form and soul, in a state of anxiety-ridden, stasis—until the hour when it is deemed acceptable to slip back once more into your true self. Whereas in a hotel, aside from the annoyance and irritation of checking-in, you are free to come and go as you please and the facilities are there to be used freely (even if you have to pay for them), in a B&B the experience is far more prescribed: your movements are monitored, there are places you cannot go, times at which you should be absent, an understanding that you will have to engage with your host on a far more intimate level every time you encounter them.

The proprietors of B&Bs are usually intrusive and ill-mannered beyond reason. They ask shockingly personal questions with apparent impunity. If there is something you would rather not talk about, well that is precisely the thing they will want to thrash out with you, and at great length. Whatever the reason for showing up in their locality must be provided in excruciating detail before they deign to hand over the keys. Before you can get the miniature kettle going. Before you unleash that cheap singular biscuit left in the tiny wicker basket and go searching for the remote control to a television offering two or three channels at most.

This latest place was truly the lowest of the low. Every hotel in our price bracket was booked up for the weekend. As were all the Guest Houses. The B&Bs were all that remained and this one was the most reasonably priced of the bunch. Located at the end of a long journey of winding country roads ruled by slow moving tractors, and after many wrong turns and screaming matches between driver and co-pilot through the sprawling suburbs, we located our destination along a dimly lit cul-de-sac. From the moment we pulled up outside, I knew it would be bad: the sign advertising 'Briarville' was almost entirely obscured by a strange colored lichen. The outside light on the porch was as weak as a teenager's promise and flickered unapologetically. The doorbell didn't work. We pounded on the door with our fists and rolled our eyes to heaven and snarled at each other under the very unflattering circumstances of exhaustion and peevishness.

The proprietress Maureen opened up with a smile that had been repurposed from some other expression, mild irritation perhaps. We were an hour late! The light in the hallway was dimmer than the one on the porch and under its grimy glaze she looked a little older than you might expect from someone running a B&B in their home. Grandmotherly. A stumble away from the nursing home. Initially, she fooled us with the sweet old lady routine. In fact, she had us eating from the palm of her wrinkly hand from the moment we checked in. Knowing we had driven for three hours and it being late at night, she did not detain us any longer than was necessary. By that I mean ten minutes of rapid-fire questioning. A grimace indicated when she had heard enough, and we were handed the keyring and discretely pointed up the noisy wooden stairs of this very small, terraced house to a room in which, never mind swinging a cat, try swinging a kitten, we were greeted by a smell of underarm deodorant and desiccated pot pourri.

It was too late to find somewhere else to stay. We were stuck here for the weekend. I tried to move around with my bags, as did my wife, and we were stuck there and jostling against each other, apologizing, arguing, and trying to get the door behind us closed so that we could have a proper full-blown argument inside the room and not out on the landing.

It was an absolute dump of a room. The sheets and pillows were clean but had been laundered to a state of near transparent flimsiness. The faded wooden bed frame groaned arthritically with every stress placed on it. In the corner of the room was a fairy door concealing an ensuite bathroom that was impossible to inhabit, the dimensions of which defied reality, indeed failed to meet the very definition of 'space'. Stains on the miniature mirror, stains on the wardrobe, stains on the carpet, stains everywhere in a room that had hosted every creed of beleaguered guest since the dawn of creation. Again an issue with the lighting: one weak bulb in a tasselled and battered light shade. No better time for my wife and I to have a rollicking row. What was it about our relationship that had brought us to this place, of all places? Just for once can we splash out and stay somewhere half decent. Hold on, I thought we'd agreed to save our money for a deposit. Oh, here we go again, the deposit, the deposit...

The many difficulties facing us inflated to an almost insurmountable degree with respect to our shared happiness. The notion (or myth) of shared happiness was compounded by the absence of a remote control to change the channel on a television positioned so high that viewing would require neck surgery beyond five-minute intervals. Despite our rule to the contrary, we decided to go to sleep without having first "made-up" with the festering allowed to continue when our buttocks touched briefly and were bilaterally withdrawn. For the sake of a little bit extra, we could have stayed in a three-star hotel, she said with finality.

I pretended to be asleep.

When it did make an appearance, sleep was a fitful companion who came and went at will between the countless bizarre and lucid nightmares playing non-stop against the backdrop of my skull. At 6.15 AM I heard a neighboring guest depart the B&B. That's what my illuminated watch-face told me. How anyone would be expected to sleep through the loud reverberations caused by human beings in this uninsulated abode was completely beyond me. As if that wasn't bad enough, the neighboring room was then attacked by the cleaner at precisely 8.01 AM while we lay there, right next door, enjoying our well-earned Saturday morning lie-in.

The message coming loud and clear from the owner of the B&B was that she had absolutely no regard for her guests. Having asked the cleaner why she was cleaning before any suitable check-out time she stated (as if it were self-evident) that she had been instructed to do so by the proprietress. The inference, that I picked up on, through her not-so-subtle demeanour and facial expressions, was that I was one of those 'awkward types' to be questioning her at this hour of the morning. She was under pressure to get rooms ready and the slight inconsiderate matter of guests still being in bed was completely irrelevant.

Having foregone washing any part of my body including my teeth, I was met downstairs by the same maid. She gave me a basket of stale bread, old croissants in plastic, and a sachet of coffee. She said "Enjoy!" in such a way that when translated it became "I hope you choke!" I then asked if she was going to take my order for breakfast and she said, "You're not having breakfast," which was at least an admission that what she had handed me did not meet the definition of breakfast. How she had come to this conclusion was something of a mystery considering that this was a B&B, and the usual thing included in the price of the stay is to receive a cooked breakfast of sausage, rasher, egg, tomato, mushrooms, toast, and tea/coffee or at least to be offered some alternative such as scrambled eggs on toast, eggs benedict, or even a bowl of porridge.

It had nothing to do with her. A breakfast order had to be placed the night before, if required by a guest, for the following morning. And how pray-tell was I supposed to know that this was the rule? A little laugh of exasperation from the lady. It was pinned on the back of the door in our room, clearly legible in bold caps and laminated. If there was a problem I would have to take it up with the owner. When I demanded to speak with the owner, I was informed that she was still in bed since no orders had been received for breakfast.

I sulked at the little table in the breakfast room and resolved to stay there until my breakfast arrived. The cleaner departed and I heard the vacuuming re-start upstairs.

When the proprietress did descend, with heavy steps and sour face, it was arm in arm with my wife. They had managed to enact a proper getting-to-know-you encounter on the upstairs landing and were now firm friends. The proprietress first wanted to know how old I thought she was. Go on and have a guess. How old did I think she was? (More accurately how old did I think she looked?) I would have guessed at somewhere around eighty-five to ninety years of age. I made the figure sixty-nine come out of my mouth, after a long series of humming and hawing noises. Our host smiled with satisfaction and then informed us that she was actually eighty-four years old and while waiting to bask in the glow of our exclamations of astonishment—I noticed the first hint of a glint in her eye.

We had to help her with something on her tablet device. It was a flustering breathless display now that I think on it critically. She was using us as her helpers. She was due to fly out somewhere for a week and the bus to the airport needed to be booked, but the time escaped her, the name of the bus company escaped her, the only thing she did know was that one of her old cronies would be on the bus and she wanted to take the same bus as her. We were put to work checking the names, times, dates of her itinerary while talking to a complete stranger on the phone to make all the necessary arrangements for her holiday in the sun.

Halfway through this cacophonous, messy, over-and-back waste of our time—another man entered the house and was introduced jokingly as her toy-boy. He seemed good-natured enough and began to involve himself in the proceedings until there were three adults trying to arrange her affairs without knowing exactly what we were supposed to be doing. After nearly an hour of this farcical carry-on I insisted that we had to be somewhere. The funeral that we had travelled all the way to attend was still to be located in an unfamiliar part of the city. I had to wrest the tablet from my wife's hands and make our apologies before dragging her out of the private living area and into the car.

I won't describe the row we had on the way there. I'm not good with maps or directions, or one-way streets, or cyclists and also Colleen wanted to discuss our financial arrangements, and the interest rates on our various personal loans. She had been talking to Maureen about it, and Maureen had told her to consolidate all the loans into one big loan and then to go to the nearest building society and every week to deposit a thousand and take out two thousand and then... blah, blah, blah. I was naturally enough furious that our private money matters had been discussed in some detail with a complete stranger. Colleen has a very trusting nature. Too trusting in my opinion, but who am I to have an opinion when the financial mess we were in was all of my fault, apparently.

We made it to the funeral. The woman (an acquaintance we had not seen or heard from in many years) had been killed off her bicycle by a tractor and trailer, having retired only a week before. A whole unfettered life of hobbies and minding grandchildren all laid out before her. Retirement from the graver responsibilities of life. Her own children raised. Investments all sound. Great pension. Nothing to worry about. Then all over. Freak accident. Unbelievable. So many people crying at the funeral. She was a wonderful person and a true credit to her family. The entire cathedral was full of well-wishers because she had been such a decent soul and deserved to live a longer and a happier life. That's what we overheard some people saying afterwards at the reception in the marquee. There was a full buffet dinner and a free bar. I recognized a lot of old faces and spent the time telling my wife about their individual situations in life. We embraced her shell-shocked husband and commiserated as best we could. We paid our respects and we felt good about the fact that her husband thanked us repeatedly for coming so far for the funeral. He said it was good of us. We thought so too.

Late in the evening we returned to the B&B in an understandably subdued mood to rest up and then travel home early in the morning.

Maureen was waiting for us by the stairs. Had she remained standing there all day? Who knows. She was well up for a bit of a chin wag. There was a photograph on the wall of her extended family. All beautiful children and grandchildren in the whiteness of some heavenly inspired photographer's studio with everyone wearing white clothes so that they were like dead people in a memory. As we were introduced to each angel individually I lapsed into an impromptu daydream of my being employed as her lackey. I'd grown a large ugly moustache and put on so much weight that my necktie would not reach down to my belt. The eternity we would spend together would only be broken in the traditional sense by some kind of hero releasing me from the spell. My wife as hero, would hack through the overgrown brambles, past the signs warning trespassers, and release me by defeating the evil crone in a hoovering contest.

"You haven't been listening to a single word we've been saying," said my wife. She was perfectly correct, and I was not about to start dancing now, either. I just stood there, staring at the carpet, stubbornly refusing to take part in their conversation and to perform the role that had been earmarked for me. I was not going to behave like a dancing bear for them; if anything I was a wild animal and demanded to be treated as one. Colleen was furious and so annoyed by my rudeness in front of Maureen that she felt obliged to apologize for my behavior and to blame it on the difficult day we'd endured. When Maureen wished us a good night and merged into the wallpaper, my wife dealt me a vicious blow to the arm and called me various obscene names.

Colleen then bounded up the stairs and slammed the bedroom door. As I trooped slowly up in her wake to begin round two, I was surprised by her pushing past me to come straight back down again, presumably to find the old dear and have a good gripe about my dreadful manners and insulting attitude which she was mortified about and simply could not fathom. Up in the bedroom I worked hard to control my anger despite the overwhelming urge to roar through this little house, smashing every breakable object before kicking the front door off its hinges. Instead I lay down, opened my book, and read a few lines before placing it open across my face so that I could smell the paper and the adhesive used to bind the pages. Gradually my anger subsided to its normal baseline, and I even managed to fall asleep.

Colleen fell into the room at two in the morning reeking of white wine and repentant. "A nutter, isn't she?" before launching into an abridged version of her evening with the old woman in her private quarters. After the second or third glass of cheap wine, Colleen had realized she was being pumped for information by the old madam and that things were taking a turn for the worst. "She actually refers to herself as an expert in pain," giggled my dear drunk wife, before vomiting on the pillow and falling asleep hugging a small plastic bin.

In the morning, it was left to me to face the dragon. I informed her that we did not want a breakfast of any description whatsoever, but she steadfastly insisted that she provide us with something small for our long journey home, something continental, such as lukewarm coffee and a choice of cereals, stored for God knows how long, in great plastic drums acquired at a once upon a time Tupperware party.

As I pushed the notes into her hand and thanked her for providing such a lovely place to rest our weary heads for the weekend, Maureen shook her head and quoted me an entirely exorbitant price per night, far higher than what had just been handed to her. It simply wasn't possible that she could be disbelieved, owing to her quiet mater-of-fact tone, her hand still outstretched, smiling serenely, because she did tell my wife over the phone, who was waiting in the car and trying to get some badly needed sleep after hours of dry retching, that this particular weekend would be more expensive than the rates quoted on the website and furthermore she also took the opportunity to tell me that I was a perfect disgrace for causing my poor wife so much distress over our finances and that if I didn't have any regard for money, how were we ever going to be in a position to purchase our own home instead of continually renting?

What Maureen was hoping and undoubtedly expecting was a furious tirade of indignation and finger-pointing from yours truly, further evidence that I was a hot-head and not a very nice person to deal with. She is, after all an expert in pain, inflicting pain that is. Instead, I gave her a wide grin and, though inwardly trembling, paid her the extra amount without any quibble. Then, to her bewilderment, I counted out a series of additional notes insisting that she take them. For what? For loss of future bookings, and I enunciated very slowly and very deliberately, whilst maintaining eye contact, a comprehensive list of the many, many, online sites where my stinging review of her rotten B&B would stand tall, like a colossal lighthouse shooting out a powerful beam of light to warn all unsuspecting and weary travellers of the dangerous currents and jagged rocks hidden beneath the surface of Br…

She slammed the door in my face.

OBITUARY

The death has occurred of Laurence 'Larry' Reilly after a brief illness, at the age of 61. Larry is survived by his two daughters, Niamh and Regina, and by estranged wife, Pauline; he will be remembered for his role as CEO of the charity organization *Helping Hands*. *Helping Hands* had previously claimed in the High Court that its former CEO had misappropriated hundreds of thousands of euros from donations to the charity for his own, personal use. The charity, which assists farmers in developing nations through donations of livestock, had secured a temporary High Court injunction freezing his assets.

The court heard that Mr. Reilly denied all allegations of wrongdoing and protested his innocence. *Helping Hands* claimed that an internal investigation into his conduct had revealed that he was guilty of a breach of trust and an appalling dereliction of his duty to the beneficiaries. Senior counsel for *Helping Hands* said his client's investigations showed that at least €765,000 of monies donated to the charity has been misappropriated by Mr. Reilly, and the figure could be much higher. Counsel said in order to conceal his wrongdoing, Mr. Reilly had also contrived requests from the missions and forged receipts, purporting to vouch payment of those funds. *Helping Hands* believes the projects in Rwanda were falsified, and it does not know what was done with those funds.

Last year, *Helping Hands* began an internal investigation into various irregularities regarding how the charity was being run. Counsel said it is their case that Mr. Reilly did not co-operate with the investigations regarding the alleged misconduct. Arising out of his non-co-operation he was suspended from his role as CEO and resigned from his post in February. Counsel said that, as far as *Helping Hands* are concerned, the resignation was an attempt to prevent various matters from being uncovered.

Some of the allegations made against him included: deleting vast swathes of data from the computer his employer had provided him; forging documents to cover his tracks; betraying the trust and confidence which the board had placed in him; conspiring with others to have a former chairperson removed from his position after an investigation into his conduct was raised; even barricading himself into an office and activating the fire alarm to escape questioning.

Pauline, his widow, served as a wonderful wife and supported him emotionally through thick and thin. They produced two devoted children who loved him—and he destroyed it all by getting involved with a Belarussian pole-dancer on the eve of his fifty-seventh birthday on a night-out with the Board of Directors. Within a month, he was supporting her financially by allowing her to live rent-free in his city centre rental property. She moved her mother and brother into the apartment and then demanded that Larry pay for her college education. When she decided not to complete the course, she asked for a car and was given the use of a *Helping Hands* company vehicle which she subsequently sold for cash. Despite all the advice his friends gave him, Larry refused to cut ties with Magda and was soon embroiled in a court battle over her allegations that he had become abusive towards her.

When she fell pregnant, he was forced to bring legal proceedings against her to establish paternity. The outcome of the paternity test proved beyond any doubt that he was not the father of the child—at which point he completely lost his head and decided to adopt the child as his own. Magda finally put a stop to the whole thing and admitted that she did not want to have anything to do with him, acknowledging that she had been using him for money and that she had never loved him. It is believed (by me) that the money he misappropriated from *Helping Hands* subsidized Magda to raise her child in a comfortable manner just outside Grodno. Thrown out of his home and paying way over the odds for a rental property, he lived a solitary life towards the end, during which time he took up candle-making and violin lessons to while away the hours. I considered myself a friend of Larry's, not just a work colleague, right up to the point where the truth finally blundered out into the open. It was only at that point that I realized how little I knew about the real person lurking behind the pillar-of-the-community facade.

He lied straight to my face and swore on the lives of his two girls that it was all an orchestrated witch-hunt against him. By whom? I asked. He shook his head and told me with that same unwavering supercilious manner of his that I was being naïve. I'm trying to think of a story that will somehow give you the true essence of Larry as an individual, as a real person, as opposed to the usual bland outline of where he was born, where he went to school, what he achieved, etc. What did he achieve? Who was he? What did he see as his purpose in life? I don't know. How did he think he would get away with it? I have no idea. Nothing about him can be taken at face value. I was used the same way he used everyone else in *Helping Hands,* and yet now they come crying to me, certain individuals from the Board of Directors, individuals whose names shall remain nameless, and they expect me to pull together something kind and respectful. An official statement from the organization to be read out at the service to draw a line under his misappropriation.

His cancer made him intensely happy towards the end of his life because it gave him the freedom to demand the attention of anyone who knew him, even remotely, and because he was so seriously unwell, it somehow absolved him, at least in his own mind, of the disgraceful way he'd conducted himself. I know it's unseemly to speak ill of the dead but on the news of his passing, *Helping Hands* held a minute's silence that did not last anywhere near the full minute. A brief pause, then everyone carried-on as before. There were quite a few people in the organization who were not displeased by the news, and the manner of his passing was noted with an unspoken satisfaction by some. My initial loyalty to him has no doubt colored me in the eyes of those same people; I might not get another opportunity to regain their trust. It prompted me to say what I felt needed saying.

Helping Hands has introduced a suite of financial policies including a robust bequest and legacy policy with checks and balances to improve our financial procedures and ensure best practices.

As mentioned earlier he is survived by his estranged wife and two grown-up children. What else is there to say about the man? I don't know. Let God be the judge. How about that? Only He truly knows what Larry was thinking: the rest of us can all go to hell. The funeral service will be held at South Lake Crematorium, Rowan Road at 12 pm. Although all are welcome to attend, we ask you to please respect the privacy of the family at this difficult time. All donations to *Helping Hands* should be through the official website only. No flowers, please.

LUCIDITY AND THE ART OF MIME

The phenomenon referred to as *Terminal Lucidity* is when a dying person who has been largely indifferent and taciturn suddenly becomes alert and coherent seemingly out of nowhere. It's a temporary condition and can last for hours or even, in some cases, a few days. There are various explanations provided, but the truth is, no one really knows why it happens. In the case of Paul Dunning, what made things even more interesting was that his lucidity took the form of a six-inch-tall, imaginary childhood companion. My understanding of what happened is that a little woodland sprite leapt onto his desk, shouted "What are *you* doing here?" and after looking around with obvious distaste, continued: "This is a right depressing kip, isn't it!"

Such was the obvious surprise and shock of seeing this little creature that the poor man immediately stopped what he was doing and forced himself to take a long critical survey of his immediate workspace. He was forced to concede that the sprite was perfectly correct: he was in a dark place in every possible sense, from the low wattage lightbulb to allowing himself be entrapped in a dull and futile existence, distanced from work colleagues because of a complete want for the most basic social skills and emboldened by his waspish and sarcastic tongue into a life of self-imposed solitude.

"Are they keeping you here against your will?" asked the naked little creature as he scratched his bottom and simultaneously picked his nose.

The sprite (Lucidity) genuinely could not begin to understand the rationale behind Paul Dunning's continued presence in this dank little hovel on the outskirts of civilization. Dunning was forced to explain that he had bills to pay every month, without fail. He listed all of these out using a wagging finger for each one: electricity, gas, rubbish, mortgage, car loan, to name but a few. The sprite listened with the false impression that this was all very interesting. He held one elbow and stroked his chin, nodding along with each iteration; then turned on a sixpence, declaring, "Remember when you used to say you would never allow yourself to become a dull middle-aged mediocrity..." and then emphatically, "have a good long look in the mirror, Paul!"

The great secret buried deep in his soul: Paul was a quite brilliant mime artist. Or at least had once possessed all the raw talent to become truly brilliant. Entirely self-trained, his early forays into the competitive world of mime had slammed him against an imaginary brick wall, but instead of bouncing back as most mimes do—he quit miming there and then in a fit of pique—walked away from the whole thing, wiping away imaginary tears. His parents and sisters had never known of his secret forays into mime and assumed that his moodiness was an entirely well-known side effect of the teenage condition.

Dunning had come to the bitter conclusion that his life was now halfway over and he had absolutely nothing to show for it. Aside from a middle-of-the-road car. Aside from a mortgage well-down-the-road towards being paid off. Aside from a lovely coffee maker. But no wife, or children, or friends, or adulation from the world of mime—all the things that really matter in life and give it some kind of meaning.

The sprite jumped up onto his desk sending his biros and pencils rolling across the desk and spilling to the ground. He log rolled on a HB pencil with a malicious expression on his face. It was clear that his words had wounded Paul and now he planned to ram home his advantage by performing the classic *rope-pulling mime* and made quite a fine job of it too. Dunning decided to ignore him. In his experience, ignoring a problem made it go away. He slouched back on his office chair and typed on his keyboard, composing a long series of cutting remarks in a furious tirade of abuse, aimed at those below him in the pecking order. The sprite was impatiently tapping his foot with arms crossed. Wasn't going to be quite as easy to break this one as he had first thought.

He hopped up onto Dunning's shoulder to get a closer look at the computer screen and to scrutinise what was being typed by a bad tempered and now heavily perspiring employee in a medium-sized, heavily state-subsized home heating engineering specialists firm that provided both solid fuel and gas heating solutions to both the commercial and residential sectors since 1987. It was a great employer in the area, especially for the native speakers—who had so few opportunities on this side of the city—and were damn glad of a job to support their growing families of native speakers.

"Are you truly happy working here?" asked the little chap.

Mr. Dunning seriously considered the question and was almost going to answer the sprite but delayed his response in order to come up with something pithier, something hard-nosed, something to kill the argument dead. It was not really so simple as saying, black or white, yes or no—it needed to be teased out a little bit more fully than that. Happiness was hardly a concept that could be freed from the cage so easily and allowed to just roam unhindered. Rather it was a wild animal that needed to be tamed and stroked and then put to sleep when—but he was rudely interrupted by a poisonous piping voice:

"Do not give me that *I'm not un-happy* line or I will climb deeper inside your ear and really start kicking off," warned the little mite.

When Dunning, once again reverted to typing furiously, the sprite squeezed himself deeper inside the waxy earhole of his large friend and began to make an unholy racket shouting and roaring as loud as his little lungs allowed. Dunning was so put off his work by the sprite that he made a complete hames of the detailed spreadsheet he was working on and then neglected to save it correctly, thereby losing all the important data he had been collating that morning. There was no chance he could update all the user specifications in the timeframe allocated to him. Frankly, it would require a complete re-population that would devour so much of his time as to put him behind schedule on the built-in functional reboot project. What possible excuse could he provide to his line manager to explain the ripple effect of delays caused by his imaginary childhood friend appearing out of the blue after thirty years?

"Jesus Christ, sprite—will you ever just leave me alone!"

The sprite emerged, covered in earwax, and gazed up at him. Shaking his little head at something truly pitiful, the sprite remembered someone very different: a kid with a wild streak and a pronounced cow's lick who was never happy unless he was doing something bold. Like the time he jumped onto the back of a donkey to see if he could hold on and was so nearly kicked to death; like the time he almost burned down his parent's house when messing around with cans of kerosene; like the time he almost broke his hip running naked down the street from a stag party gone horribly wrong not to mention the consequent police investigation. It all seemed so long ago. This greying middle-aged man bore no resemblance to his friend of years ago. This guy was a dull, respectable, fraud.

Dunning watched the sprite walk away, head hanging low, and was perfectly willing to let him go—until he realized that the little git had stolen his wallet, car keys, and mobile phone. Paul hurried outside to see where the sprite had taken his stuff, but he was gone and so too were his personal items. The outside air made him feel queasy. It was the first time in many years that Dunning had been outside of his basement level office at this hour of the day; the intensity of the daylight actually hurt his eyes. It felt uncanny out here; he was even a little frightened to be above ground without his manager's written consent. His reflection in the window of a nearby parked car revealed a gaunt shouldered man with a heavily bearded face disguising two moist, rapidly blinking eyes. It took Paul a few painful moments to finally reconcile that ugly reflection to himself.

Wait, wasn't that the little sprite over yonder, leaping effortlessly over a low stone wall by a telegraph pole, and then ducking in the tall grass!

If he wanted his personal items back, he would need to pursue the sprite. To surprise the little thief, he stumbled forward, his legs describing a wide arc, to creep up on his old friend. Grab him around the neck and squeeze the life out of him was the full extent of his plan. While stumbling over the uneven ground, he had to contend with tormenting reminders of the inner child buried inside him: a small boy playing under the enormous fully mature oak trees behind his house that were subsequently pulled down to build more houses, indulging in some fantastic solo adventure in which he was the hero, and this was generally understood by everyone. It was out there on the wasteland behind his house that a friendship had been formed with a small woodland creature.

Naturally, he never told anyone about the sprite. He wasn't stupid; he knew that the creature was magical. The sprite had encouraged him to fully give himself over to the art of mime and provided him with critical feedback on all aspects of the 'work' as he called it. Over time, Paul felt his confidence growing and blossoming under the tutelage of his diminutive mentor until that horrible experience at the regional mime exposition mentioned earlier. After that traumatic event, little Paul spent less and less time out in the wasteland using the excuse of having too much homework and football training and birthday parties and visits to the dentist and a whole myriad of other banal commitments. He had stopped wanting and needing the sprite's tuition, and the sprite had got the message.

So why was he back now? After all these years. What was it about his life that required the little creature's intervention? Everything was motoring along as it should be as far as he was concerned. There were no major crises on the immediate horizon. Nothing had happened either in his personal or professional life to warrant the reappearance of this imaginary childhood character. Fine, the little man had revealed the emptiness and shallowness of his life but so what? It was too late to do anything about it now. What concerned Paul was that this reappearance could perhaps herald the arrival of something far more damaging from a psychological frame of mind. Was there perhaps a hint of an upcoming mid-life crisis or partial mental breakdown with mind-numbing medication for dessert?

Mr. Dunning eventually found the sprite in a clearing. The contents of his wallet were strewn across the ground. His receipts, having been tossed around in the breeze, were stuck to the outstretched fingers of the surrounding bushes and shrubs. His ID cards were spread out on the earth like a deck of playing cards. The sprite was playing some game with them, sitting cross-legged atop an overhanging dandelion. Totally immersed in the activity of matching the cards into pairs, he paid no attention to the heavily perspiring man breathing heavily and bearing down on him. Dunning saw that his expensive phone had been dismantled piece by piece and his car keys hung around the sprite like a necklace.

He reached out ready to grab and choke. But of course, the closer he got, the louder his blundering approach, and the sprite without looking said:

"I hope you're not planning to kill me, Paul!"

Dunning lunged forward to capture the sprite and, closing his eyes, was stung all over his hands by the bunch of nettles he persisted in shaking angrily, throwing to the ground and stomping on. All the while he was emitting a bizarre series of expletives and removing every item of clothing from his body.

It was at this point that we tried to coax him back inside the factory, at least until the ambulance could take him away, but he insisted that he was trapped inside a large, transparent, multi-planar labyrinth. The dimensions of this labyrinth in which Paul found himself imprisoned were quite staggering to behold. Word spread and in time everyone in the plant filed out to watch him explore the walls of the maze and rebound theatrically against them, examining the full extent of every plane, and uncovering every corridor, closed door, every window, every stairwell leading up and down, every table and chair, every item of food that had been laid out for him with each bite producing a new facial expression: bitter, sweet, hot, cold, you name it he tasted it, and afterwards a lie-down on an imaginary bed and then exaggerated yawning and stretching before restful sleep.

It was a performance that will live long in the memory of each and every one of us standing there in the lashing rain on that otherwise dull Tuesday afternoon in June. You ask why I'm bringing this up all these months later? Well, I saw him yesterday for the first time since that momentous day, crossing the street in old, ill-fitting clothes, his shoelaces undone and trailing behind him, a beanie hat pulled down over dreadlocks, and a voluminous unkempt beard. He didn't notice me at first because he was too busy muttering to himself about something or other while describing the problem with his two hands supporting an invisible object hovering at about eye level.

The other thing. I did mention two things, you're right, Karen. It is Karen, isn't it? Yes, I got side-tracked talking about—well, you see, it's not good news frankly, but as some of you may know, especially if you have purchased shares in the company, the markets are trending down, sales are soft for the quarter, plus with the whole move to renewable sources of energy... so what I'm trying to say is that we've taken the difficult decision to reduce down to a three-day working week. Starting from next Monday. I know there were rumours. It's terrible news. It's a bugger. I hate to be the bearer of such bad news and late on a Friday evening but there you are. No, that's all I've been told. It's purely a business decision at the end of the day. Management looked at all the other ways to save money and cut costs and this was the only possible way forward, sadly.

Look guys I see the long faces—it's not the end of the world. Really and truly, it could be worse. For instance you could be out of a job and aimlessly roaming the streets describing some great conspiracy and nobody will so much as give you the time of day. He actually recognised me and convinced me to go for coffee with him to explain what happened. The strange part is that he seemed so much happier when I met him than anytime when he worked here. I mean he was friendly, relaxed, and completely candid about his episode. He said it was the best thing that ever happened to him—that it really 'opened him up'. He wanted you all to know that he has started a podcast where the proof of his various conspiracy theories about capitalism are fully detailed. I had a listen. It's kind of interesting, if you're into that kind of thing.

Oh yes, I almost forgot to tell you about the best part. Just out of curiosity, to try and draw him out, I asked him if he had remained in contact with the sprite, or if it had gone away again after the episode. Next thing his beanie hat starts jigging around on his head, and I hear this high-pitched little voice call me every obscene name under the sun. Dunning pulls it off and starts to wrestle it into submission and squeeze it under his armpit, offering me a mortified expression of his embarrassment, before hurriedly taking his leave.

Anyway, I hope you're not worried about your jobs. You will have plenty of time to make an informed decision if there is to be a round of redundancies—and I'm not saying there will be—that decision has yet to even be considered, so I wouldn't worry. My advice would be to stay here and see what happens. There's talk about a private equity firm possibly being interested—again I don't know anything about that. It may never happen. If you do have questions you can contact me. My door is always open. Unless I'm in a meeting. Does that make sense? Any questions? I'll take your silence as a No.

DEADBEATS

A crisis meeting had been scheduled to discuss their short and long-term goals. Would they continue to make critically acclaimed but commercially unsuccessful music or willingly pander to an audience that appreciated a poppier sound, a softer, more melodic approach? Mark understood that he should be in attendance to properly influence proceedings, to stamp out the plotting against him, but he was otherwise engaged. Whining and self-pity would segue into blaming him for their perceived lack of success and would finally settle into a long dreary silence. It would necessitate him standing up and delivering yet another impassioned defence of their abrasive sound and image. Without their signature abrasive sound and image, there was no attitude, and if there was no attitude they might as well be a third-rate pub band. Couldn't they see that for themselves! As the anointed founding member of The Deadbeats this was what they looked to him for, this restatement of their vision, every time the wheels threatened to come off.

His having missed yet another rehearsal would be used as further evidence against him. Further evidence for a supposed lack of direction as far as his bandmates were concerned. Lately Mark kept finding obscure reasons for not showing up, providing no excuses to his bandmates, and treating their tentative suggestions with withering contempt. His band was not a democracy; he would rather walk away than take on board the frivolous suggestions offered by a half-deaf drummer and his half-wit bassist brother. They were the main agitators for change; the other two were too smart to say anything directly to Mark, instead they looked at the ground or at the ceiling when asked how they felt about things.

What made matters worse was that the cashier serving him in that over-bright department store was annoying and over-familiar. She wanted to verbalize every moment of their interaction in minute detail: "put that in a bag for you" and "just slot that into the machine" and "oh, seems to be a bit of a problem here… these things can be a bit slow…just try your pin again." He was attempting to buy a Communion dress for his daughter, having completely forgotten that tomorrow was her big day. She would not be able to make her First Communion without the customary angelic white dress. However Mark was unable to pay for it because the machine repeated that there was a problem with his card and that he should contact his bank every time she tried to put it through.

Obviously some mistake. Some error on their end. Used the card earlier on (a lie). Not to worry. Back in a few minutes. Tilts her head to one side, a look of recognition lights up her formerly vacant little face, asks if he plays with the Deadbeats. Fake eyelashes batting like birds' wings. Literally like their biggest fan. When are they gigging again? Next week in Toner's, he could put her on the guest list. What's her name? What's her number? Bit on the young side. Still, cute enough. Uncertain twist to her mouth. A brief grimace that he chooses to ignore. He puts her into his phone. Nice to meet you too, Sally. She's going on her break, actually. Stick the dress out back in the storeroom for him. Thanks a million Sally. Just in case she's not there when he comes back for it.

Mark slotted his useless bank card back inside his empty wallet, and went out outside. To his surprise, the sun had come out and everyone was walking around in T-shirts, shorts, short dresses, and flip-flops. As always, he was dressed entirely in black: black jeans, black shirt, black leather jacket, black socks, big chunky black boots. The sound of traffic and people walking through the streets came at him in a wave as soon as the automatic doors parted. He was soon roasting in the leather jacket. He took it off and threw it over his shoulder, hanging it off his curled-up index finger. Where was his nearest branch? A mind map extending out in every direction, of every branch that was no longer open, signs pulled down and converted to coffee shops or trendy barbers. Why were there so many trendy barbers around town? How was it sustainable? Then again, the beard was back in fashion and all the trimming that involved. Stood to reason.

The cashier at his friendly local branch still open to customers explained from behind thick Perspex that to access monies from a savings account would require at least three working days' notice. She held out a thin slip of paper for him to complete. As much as she wanted to help him out there was simply nothing she could do to transfer the funds from one account to another at such short notice. His current account currently amounted to twelve euros and forty-seven cents. She circled the amount with her red biro.

What was that about?

There was no need to get angry with her—she was just doing her job. Sorry he felt that way.

Next!

If he wanted to make a formal complaint that was his prerogative. He could speak to the Branch Manager, of course he could.

Waste of time. A knob jockey with a mouthful of veneers and a snide manner. Terms and Conditions. Could get him a copy of them if he so desired.

Sorry he felt that way but no need to get personal.

Outside the bank Mark slid on his aviator shades to hide his eyes from the daylight.

THINK!

Checked his phone. The Social Welfare office would be open. They still owed him. Denied his latest claim because he hadn't signed-on at their offices on the specific date allotted to him. He was entitled to that money. His stamps were all there. It was a scandal to deny someone what they were legally and rightfully entitled to. A month of missed payments would easily pay for the dress. He needed the money now.

Through a series of tight alleyways to where the new offices were located. So much better than the old place. Much more modern. A smell of newness and everything clean. Take a ticket and wait in line like everyone else. No, he was not willing to wait in line like everyone else; he was in a hurry. They were messing him around. Shouted accusations at some guy behind Perspex.

Everyone was behind Perspex when you wanted your money.

Security Guard called.

He was entitled to his money, not leaving without his money. He knew his rights.

A large man in a jumper that seemed too small for his frame came and stood next to him. Doleful eyes, almost an apologetic manner, huge meaty hands.

"Let's take this outside," said the large man in the jumper.

Mark swore at him, pretended that he wasn't intimidated by this bored-looking goon, then stormed out of the offices, glaring back at the smirking onlookers.

Fuck them!

They were no better than him, queuing up for a handout. Useless bastards.

He was a musician. What did they do all day?

Drink coffee. Have their beards trimmed.

It was complete bullshit; he was seeing red, unable to control his emotions, incapable of thinking in a rational manner about the simple problem in front of him. He needed money. It was that simple. Just borrow it from somebody and then pay them back whenever. Simple as. Except he couldn't think of even a single person that would lend him money. Every bridge had been burned in that respect.

Nip home and have a smoke. That would help calm him down. There had to be a way out of this...there had to be!

On stage Mark, had a certain tendency to lose all control of his facial expressions and close his eyes, as his fingers ran up and down the frets in a crazed manner, while his hair flopped over his eyes and his jaw clenched in concentration, as if wringing every last drop of wank out of the tip of his guitar. That was what his ex-partner pictured when she thought of him: a slightly ridiculous-looking older man playing his guitar, trapped inside some fantasy that he could still make it by sheer force of will.

She was trying to call him on his mobile phone but getting his answering machine every time.

The First Communion was tomorrow.

So where was the famous dress?

He'd promised to pay for it and collect it and drop it over to her house.

She hated the sight of him. Worse, their daughter refused to be disappointed in him, despite his constant excuses and pissy attitude to everything outside of his blinkered vision. Fuelled exclusively by a never-ending ego. He'd insisted on buying the dress, and here they were, the day before the Communion and no damn dress. Eve had spent an hour with him in the shop, picking out the specific one that she wanted, and no other dress was going to do her now because it was the one she had picked out with her dad and the one he liked the best too.

So why, oh bloody why, did he have to leave it to the very last minute? Every time. Every single time. Why did he have to insist on going right to the wire and risk something happening to spoil it for her? It was as if he did these things deliberately, just to irritate her; he was feckless and irresponsible to the nth degree. She couldn't decide if he consciously went out of his way to upset her or if it was just a by-product of his utterly selfish and self-centered attitude. Did he really have the time to think about anything other than himself? And worse than that, Eve idolized him, wanted to be a musician like him when she grew up, form her own band, conquer the world.

It was always up to her to remind him of his responsibilities and obligations to *his* daughter and yes that meant money but what she resented most was constantly being put in this situation. As if she somehow enjoyed pricking his bubble while he professed to have no idea how appalling his behavior was or how it might be perceived by others. The fact that he persisted with the whole band thing was proof of his delusion. One of life's perennial losers. He couldn't help it. He had a god-given talent for pissing off the people who might have helped him, who might have propelled him forward, and who expected their asses to be kissed, even the ones who wanted just one small kiss. Mark's integrity wouldn't allow him to bend down that low.

It was too much of a risk to take, trusting him to do the one thing he'd promised to do, so she had Eve put her jacket on and bring her to the place where she and her dad had picked out the most incredible Communion dress ever. They searched through the racks with a rising sense of anxiety that it was gone; they talked with the cashier when it couldn't be located anywhere. After a minor tantrum from Eve, it was located and then paid for when it appeared magically from the On Hold rack. Yes, it was cutting things fine. Tomorrow was the big day. They were on their way to get their hair done. Oh, they most certainly would enjoy the day.

Mark had retreated to the sanctuary of his bedroom. He knew that he really shouldn't, but he smoked a medium-strength joint, stretching his neck to look out his bedroom window at a trail of clouds in the blue sky. It looked like the vertebrae of some immense dinosaur around which seagulls were ululating in the usual fashion. They were floating up there in circles for no other reason than they could. They didn't need motivation to be seagulls. Must be so cool to be a seagull, he mused. Once upon a time he had been certain, and now he wasn't so sure. Confidence was ebbing away. You couldn't help but start to lose heart when every door shuts in your face, again and again and again. You couldn't help but lose heart when bandmates stabbed you in the back and questioned every decision you made despite the fact that you were the founder, and they hadn't a single decent idea between the lot of them.

There you go. Nothing ever lives up to your expectations. All the good shit had already been done to death. People didn't want to hear what he had to say. What did he have to say? What was left to do with the Deadbeats? Record another EP and send it out to every fucker in the country and fill up every gig with your friends? What was the point? The others wanted to write love songs and break-up songs. Whingeing rubbish like everyone else was doing. They didn't feel like the band fitted into a neat category. That's the whole point. He had tried to explain it to them, but it fell on deaf ears. They were all perfectly fine musicians, but they couldn't see the bigger picture the way he could. They didn't have a vision.

All he had was Eve. Everything else was fucked. Every relationship ended when he figured out what they wanted, or they figured out what he wanted. He knew he didn't have it as bad as other people. What about someone in a wheelchair or born with an incurable illness or suffering with a mental illness? He got all that. He knew he had it pretty good in many ways—just that things hadn't worked out the way he wanted and now he was beginning to appreciate that they never would. He didn't want to be him anymore. The joint really was not helping him to figure things out—it was bringing him down.

His phone was ringing. Her. Eve's mother. He wasn't going to talk to her while he was stoned. That would only be a head-wreck. So, he let it ring out and then read her instant text message written in caps. WHERE IS DRESS? The dress.

He still needed to come up with a plan. Someone he could borrow the money from. Some moron willing to give him...there we go. He pictured the very guy, a rich kid sycophant who came to all the gigs and had tried on numerous occasions to become Mark's friend. Well now was the time to prove his worth. Once he'd run through the spiel a few times in his head he found the guy's number on his phone saved under 'stalker' and after a brief chit-chat and how are you—Mark asked him outright for the lend of the money.

It was while he waited for his newest best buddy Darren to drop over the money ("absolutely no problem man, no questions asked, for real, sure man, on the way now in a cab") that Mark entertained himself with a daydream: looking out into the crowd, really feeling that connection, everyone getting it, everyone on the same buzz and the whole thing just like getting really intense, that girl from the department store, what was her name again, Sally, Sally nodding her head and really getting where he was coming from, exchanging a smile with her but not, you know, not being a sleazy bastard—as he continued to maintain this daft fantasy inside his head he wandered into the kitchenette of his apartment share and unexpectedly encountered his flat-mate, Nadine. They hardly ever saw each other on account of the fact that she worked nine to five in an office at something or other and he didn't, well...he didn't keep regular hours. Their meeting was terse as it happened because he'd forgotten to leave a certain something on the mantlepiece.

That time of the month already. Jesus, creeps up on you. Did he have the money? Of course he did, but he would just need to get down to the bank. Nadine turned her back to continue washing the dishes in a sink full of suds while muttering angrily under her breath. This was not what he needed right now. She was moody at the best of times. He retreated to the safety of his bedroom and closed the door. Would it be a bad idea to have another quick smoke? He didn't think so. Just until Darren made it over there. It would make listening to the guy somewhat bearable. Mark rolled up a quick one and put some music on. Yes, that was it, something trippy and repetitive to complement his state of mind.

"Aghh...doorbell!"

He carefully placed the joint in the ashtray and galloped down the stairs to meet Darren, his saviour. With the taxi pulling away in the background it was apparent that Darren was here to stay and not just dropping the money off. Mark reluctantly brought him inside and offered him a cup of tea or coffee. Darren was only too happy to accept the offer. He wanted tea. Thankfully, Nadine had vacated the kitchenette, so he could borrow one of her mugs and some of her tea bags, and even a spoon or two of her sugar, and what was a dash of milk between friends. He sat Darren down on the couch and produced the tea, the joint, and prepared for the onslaught.

Not only was Darren their biggest fan but he also contributed to an online forum championing local musicians and conducting interviews. He was wondering if he could do an interview with Mark if there was enough time. It wouldn't take long. Oh Christ not this again, thought Mark, he glanced at his phone and explained that there was a rehearsal happening that he really should look in on. Just hand over the cash already. Instead he had to consider what his thoughts were on a host of topics, including what his favourite song was and why most people only liked brain-dead pop music as opposed to serious music, you know. Could Mark come up with some interesting and arresting answer to these pointless probes from a dull but well-meaning superfan who had cash in his pocket for him?

The interview was proceeding along the usual strained lines when Nadine came into the room and after a protracted series of angry sighs, joined the interview to demand, quite rightly, that he go get the rent money. The landlord was coming over in an hour. She had just been on the phone to her. No more messing around Mark. This time she really meant it. A normally quiet person driven to clenching her fists and with two patches of red coloring her cheeks. She wasn't going to take no for an answer. It was embarrassing for everyone. Even Darren seemed cowed until he twigged that this was what he had been called into action for and produced the cash to placate the angry housemate.

"No, No, No," screamed Mark from the inside of his throbbing head, all the while nodding and grinning at the two of them. It was enough for this month but what about last month? She reckoned he hadn't paid for last month because when she checked her balance there didn't appear to be a deposit in his name, hadn't they agreed from the beginning that he should set up a direct debit instead of giving her cash all the time so that she had to go to the bank and...

Mark agreed that she was probably right. He and his friend would go right this instant to the bank and sort this matter out, once and for all. She wanted to continue berating him, but Mark indicated to Darren that they could continue the interview while walking out the door and so they bade farewell to Nadine. Time really was against him now. The department store would be closing in less than an hour, and he still did not have the money. Plus, he now had to carry this deadweight along with him.

Was he really stoned or was everyone staring at him on the street? It certainly seemed that way. Darren agreed that it did seem like everyone was staring at them as they walked past, but then he was stoned, or at least more ready to admit that he was stoned. The problem remained that Mark did not have the money to buy the Communion dress, and how was that going to be solved today? The thought occurred to him and was instantly dismissed but re-emerged over and over again, like that amusement arcade game with the things popping up and you have to hit them with a mallet, and because of his desperation he had to consider his sister.

As much as he hated to admit it—she was the only person he could think of—now that Darren had so spectacularly messed things up. They marched through the city together because Darren wanted to hang out with him, and Mark couldn't think of a way to get rid of him. Karen's office was down near the docks. A redeveloped zone with a beautiful bland skyline of kiddie's playthings: blocks stacked on other blocks and lots of glass and steel. The main point was that everything was so clean and polished. Mark hated this part of town. Soulless and full of empty-headed ghouls who did nothing but make money for their already rich nameless clients in other tax jurisdictions.

Karen was one of them. She'd have happily admitted to it too. All about the money. Every way to avoid paying tax on your earnings. She'd done well for herself. No denying that. If doing well for yourself meant wearing a suit and sitting in an office all day telling other people about their productivity rates and why they would never rise to her level in the organization, making sure to knock their confidence and tell them how shit at their jobs they were. Keep them at arm's length. Still, she was his sister. What did he have to lose? Only the love and respect of his daughter.

The receptionist at Karen's firm was a real piece of work. She wouldn't get his sister on the phone. She was with a client, apparently. He would have to call back at some later stage. Did he have a phone number he could be contacted on? Too late in the day for that. He just barged right into the office. Open plan style and all hushed bodies gliding across the carpets to glass cages. He paused at one rabbit hutch to ask for directions and was pointed to a corner office where her married name was inscribed on the silver plaque and a series of letters trailing behind it that was supposed to impress by revealing her credentials, her achievements, the years spent in lecture halls and tapping a pen against the desk as she studied for the next high bar.

She was not with someone but was talking on her phone. She raised a finger to Mark and pushed past him into the open plan office. She wanted to continue her conversation while containing him in one place. She closed him into her corner office and stood against the door on the other side. It would give him an opportunity to explore her cube. It didn't take long to do the tour. He plonked down in the chair opposite her desk, then got up and sat in her chair behind her desk surveying all before him.

In the glass wall of her office and under the right conditions, such as was the case at this time of the evening, her office wall became a huge mirror. His oversized boots, his ridiculous black jeans, all the way up to his tired shirt, the beaded amber necklace, the long hair, thinning now, no point in pretending otherwise. Better to look away and play with the executive toys on her desk, the little balls transmitting energy, all that useless bric-a-brac.

"This has to be done," he whispered to himself.

He reached out his hand and pressed it against the cold glass. There was a familiar face floating there in the glass, distorted but still recognizable staring back at him with an incredible intensity from two black orbits. Even when Mark blinked and looked away he could not remove the image from before his eyes. It was unmoving, grey-haired, with its jaw thrust out, a merciless withering contempt transmitted in the eyes. The mouth was stretching open, wider apart to reveal the rows of yellowing teeth. Tendons in his neck sprung out like elongated pillars. He watched as the pale flesh from that familiar face dissolved, leaving only the faint residue of a restless impressionable teenager staring back at him.

Sooner than he had imagined it, the reckoning would come, that was what this face was trying to tell him, with its astonished frozen expression. As the door opened and his sister entered, Mark rose and stumbled, backed away from the glass wall, mumbled his apologies.

Karen's eyes glared savagely.

He wouldn't be coming back again like this, would he?

He gave her his best sales pitch: a Communion dress, money unavailable, pay her back next week.

Karen nodded and hoped that the Communion would be fun for Eve. Send her some photographs, even.

She sounded sad and distant.

"You know something—you look so like dad, it's scary. Just around the eyes."

"Ok"

"Have you spoken to him lately?"

"No"

"He's always asking for you and how the band are doing. What's the name again…I can't quite…"

"Stop, you're killing me."

"Call him, he'd love to hear from you."

He could not say it. Put it into words. Just how angry he felt at the moment when the notes were squeezed into his hand.

It was being told that he looked like his father, that was unnecessary. She had wanted to make her position clear. The problem was that he couldn't so easily dismiss her wounding remark when he'd seen it for himself.

Outside was blindingly bright. He had sunglasses somewhere. He found them and slid them on over his eyes to conceal the dark empty sockets. His best friend was waiting for him by a bench. Darren. Sounds very like Karen. Were they all in this together? Was this all some way of getting back at him for being an artist in a world that didn't give two fucks about his voice?

Mark seemed unsteady on his feet. Almost enfeebled for some reason. Darren assisted him in the manner of a caregiver assisting a blind person. Helped him down the footpaths and across the roads by pressing all the buttons and waiting for the lights to change. Mark was acting really strangely. It was concerning that before he'd gone into the building he'd seemed like himself but since seeing his sister he was in this weird catatonic state.

Darren was beginning to wonder if it was something stronger than the joint. Maybe Mark had consumed something earlier in the day and was just coming up now. This was a bit of a drag really. He did have other things he wanted to do today. He asked Mark if it would be okay to leave him to it? Did he know where he was?

Talk to him later.

The crisis meeting was still in progress when Mark entered the rehearsal room and collapsed down into the nearest chair. He was prepared to listen. The band had made some big decisions in his absence. They seemed nervous but steadfast in taking a new direction, trying out new instruments and recording some songs that they had been working on in his absence. One voice spoke about wanting to change their audience to get more people interested, perhaps by improving their overall sound, making it crisper, sharper, less-feedback and even less...aggressive. Another voice agreed and said that lyrically the new songs were light years ahead of their previous stuff.

"Are you alright, Mark?" asked one of the Deadbeats.

"I'm fine," said Mark.

They were waiting for his feedback. He was aware that they expected him to react wildly to their suggestions, with a view to kicking him out of a band that he had started. He was aware of the vision he had for the band receding into a permanently limp, shuffling edifice in which he would be an embarrassed onlooker. For the briefest moment he could even see himself on the stage, nodding along, trapped in a chamber of jangling nonsense.

The pawn shop would be closed.

But tomorrow, bright and early, before the Communion ceremony, he would go and get it over with. He rose sullenly and packed it away in its case, firmly securing the clasps. He walked out the door without sharing anything intimate with the other Deadbeats. Instead, he wondered what time the Communion ceremony was set for, and whether he would have time to get the dress in the morning, whether he should confess his sin, whether he should go over there in person, or phone up, or send a carefully worded text message to explain why he'd fucked up, yet again?

He didn't do any of these things. Instead he tried calling the girl from the shop.

Sally.

He tried the number she'd given him and was rewarded with a bland male voice.

"The number you have dialled does not exist".

TUG OF WAR

I plunged my arm as far as the elbow into a large bin filled with ice-cube-infested water. My withered reddened hand resurfaced time after time with either a bottle or a can of the same brand of unremarkable beer. I kept telling myself that there had to be something different in the bin. There had to be something else in there for people who didn't drink unremarkable beer. I'd noticed other people drinking other brands. Where did they get them? This bin only contained the piss-poor beer. There must be other bins, I thought, but I could not see any in my vicinity, so I swallowed down the piss poor beer and floated like a ghost around the many groups of people in shorts and light dresses feigning interest in each other.

I had to find a way inside one of these groups. If they were forming a cell wall of inward facing lipid membrane, then I was a virus floating around in the soup searching for the ideal way to disrupt the operations of the cell with my presence. I would ask them if they liked to drink this really flat, tasteless beer. I would begin an argument on what beer ought to be in the large plastic bin. The event was a social barbecue for Irish immigrants in a corner of a municipal park. Burning burgers, burning sausages, burning chicken legs. An intoxicating aroma of pure burning flesh inside the continuous rolling plumes of acrid smoke.

I was looking for a start. By that, I mean I was looking for a job. I needed to make a connection with someone at this barbecue who had a job to offer or knew of someone who would be in a position to offer a job to an ungainly nineteen-year-old good-for-nothing work-shy layabout. Another mouthful of the piss poor beer dribbled down my chin. The disposable plate piled high with chicken bones and thoroughly inedible potato salad I had been holding onto for far too long disappeared over my shoulder. Why? Because one side of the tug of war was down a man. They were crying out for someone to take the strain. Wild eyes roved the crowd of onlookers, and they picked me out because of my lanky frame easily head and shoulders above everyone around me.

The anchor, thick rope coiled around his heavy-set body like an anaconda, screamed at me to dig my heels in. I was man-handled to the middle ranks where the men spoke to me in Irish. I nodded my head and spat on my hands. I hadn't a notion what they were saying, but I knew how to pull on a rope. The ground was bone dry, but I still dug in my heel as best I could and raised a little cloud of dust. Had I taken it a little easier on the piss-poor beer, I might have thought twice about what I was doing and let some other drunken fool take the strain, but hindsight is a told-you-so-bore who has never done anything worth mentioning.

It was only as the rope went taut that I began to realize how avidly the men on either side of the red bandana despised each other. Later I was to learn that most of the participants hailed from adjoining parishes back home with a lengthy shared history of mutual loathing. Insults had already started to fly like arrows over and back. With a countdown from the assembled crowd and a roar of appreciation, began a tug of war that would go on for hours, years, months, decades, millennia, longer than the longest ice age, longer than the creation of the universe. Why? Because I instantly needed a piss. Neither side would relinquish. Not an eighth of an inch. We were deep rooted trees clamped to the earth. Then the steady rhythmic chant through gritted teeth and straining muscles, tearing tendons, rupturing ligaments: "PULL! PULL! PULL! PULL!.........PULL!........"

My first job was set up for me by my uncle. I really had no clue what we were doing. It seemed foolish or at least unnecessary to ask, because as far as the guy I was working for was concerned, it was completely self-evident. We were in a deserted shopping mall putting a framework of steel studs into place onto which sheets of gypsum board would later be screwed and plastered to create internal walls. I had to come to my own conclusions around what we were doing there because the man I was working for (did I ever get his name?) was not very interested in the subtleties of conversation or in the subtleties of anything for that matter. All I needed to concern myself with was the accurate cutting of lengths of steel stud and then handing those lengths of stud to the sweating stranger balancing precariously on the top step of his shaky metal step ladder.

Christ almighty I couldn't even do that much right! My cutting was to prove wildly inaccurate, leaving rough edges, making the length of stud still too long for the specified location. It ended up with me passing him the cutting tool as well as the length of stud so that he could complete the cutting. The lengths I had gone to were not good enough for him. While watching him toil up on his ladder in the incredible heat, sweating, cursing, having to do his job and mine—I tried to appear sympathetic to his needs and made a number of shoulder shrugs and pained facial expressions to explain my ineptitude.

Part of the problem, as I saw it, was that he insisted on calling out the lengths in feet and inches, the imperial system, when from the very beginning of my education, the metric system was all we'd learned about. I didn't know the first thing about feet or about inches. I tried to explain this to him, but he kept calling out the measurements in feet and inches and divisions of these so that I was forced to guess—to make valiant attempts at meeting his requirements. To be fair to the guy, he did try and read off the measurements in centimeters and millimeters for a short while, but it was like a bad taste in his mouth every time he did it, like he was chewing on licorice; without any prior warning he started again spitting out feet and fractions of inches. Another part of the problem was that he was a friend of my uncle, so he couldn't bawl me out and deride me the way he would a useless good-for-nothing stranger. The poor guy was seething up there on his ladder.

Many tense and unhappy hours later, he informed me that he wouldn't be requiring my services the next day. By the time I got back to the apartment, I was informed that my services would not be required any day thereafter. My uncle upbraided me in a controlled voice, he was thoroughly ashamed of my conduct; in America he explained, you have work hard, not just show up, not just stand around with your hands in your pockets, not just...he whacked his walking stick off the wall, the rule in this country was that you worked your ass off for everything! I mulled it over while sticking to his leather couch in the sweltering heat. My getting fired reflected badly on him. I tried to make myself as physically small as I could by retreating inside my shell and keeping my mouth firmly closed.

"PULL! PULL! PULL! PULL!.........PULL!........"

The assembled onlookers screamed and wailed and willed us not to concede an inch of ground to those other bastards. Not so much as an eight of an inch. Inches again! This was probably the most important moment of our lives. Nothing before or after would ever match the intensity and sheer magnitude of this show of strength. This was our collective raison d'être—to pull on this thick rope in a park in Queens on a Sunday afternoon with a crowd of half-drunk ex-pats foaming at the mouth, all sunburnt legs and beer bellies jiggling. This was what it all boiled down to: my conscription into a war that had nothing whatsoever to do with me.

"PULL! PULL! PULL! PULL!.........PULL!........"

We continued to pull hard on the rope separating us from oblivion. Sweat running down our backs, down our faces, into our eyes, stinging and blinding us. A sudden jittery feeling through the team. All it would take was one man to lose his footing. It was my legs that were beginning to quiver from the strain. The man behind me screamed that he would strangle the life out of me if I gave in. That he would beat me to death if I stopped pulling. That he would slit my throat if I stopped pulling. I doubt he really meant it.

"PULL! PULL! PULL! PULL!.........PULL!........"

A few days later, my uncle set me up with a construction crew in Brooklyn. I was delighted with a second chance to prove my worth. Make yourself look busy. That was his parting advice as I walked out the door and caught a bus to the subway. The subway spat me out on the street corner where my contact was already waiting, shoulders hunched, puffing on a cigarette. On our short walk to the job, he explained that it was not permissible to drink alcohol while we worked (nudge-nudge-wink-wink) because we were renovating a derelict synagogue. It was impossible to tell that it had been a place of worship because the inside of the building was a skeleton of missing floors and thin interconnecting wooden beams. I was expected to follow in the footsteps of all those crazy bastards who had gone before across those rotten beams, without a harness or safety equipment, to smash out the same rotten beams with a sledgehammer. I went up the stone stairway and glanced at the long way down onto a distant concrete floor littered with more of the splintered, sharpened, jutting, beams.

If anyone there was going to fall to their death, it would surely be me. I'm not great with heights, or with anything else for that matter. I volunteered to collect the beams down below and to drag them outside to the dumpsters. I watched in disbelief as the other guys sauntered out along them without a moment's hesitation and smashed their way along, sending beams crashing down in echoing reverberations to the darkness below our feet. What concerned me most was that many of them were rotten. Just as the flooring over them had been rotten. So how were you expected to know if what you were walking along was rotten until you put your weight on it? I was handed a sledgehammer. Take it and go out smashing. Instead, I slunk away back down the solid stone stairway trying to make myself look busy doing nothing. It didn't work.

"PULL! PULL! PULL! PULL!.........PULL!........"

One hour. I was fired after one hour. I didn't even have the sense to ask for money to get home on the train or for the hour that I'd done (not that I had actually done anything). I greeted the news of my dismissal with total agreement and made no fuss whatsoever. Trudging in the apartment door my uncle greeted me with a look of incredulity and silent fury. I emphasized the danger of what I had been asked to do to win his sympathy, and it worked to some extent, I think. What I know for certain is that if I had attempted to walk out along one of those beams, I would have fallen straight down and would either have been killed or suffered life-changing injuries.

My uncle was no longer prepared to make any more phone calls on my behalf. It was time to do some of the donkey work for myself. A bunch of people were attending a barbecue in aid of some cause, I forget what it was, and I could go there and work up the courage to ask if anyone knew anyone looking for someone. I didn't like the sound of this idea one little bit, but I couldn't tell my uncle that. No, I had to agree that it was up to me to make things happen, to go out there and sell myself. He was right—it was ridiculous for a healthy young man to sit around watching daytime television when he'd flown the whole way over here to make money. I would go to the barbecue. I would do whatever it took.

"PULL! PULL! PULL! PULL!.........PULL!........"

Every sinew stretched beyond its point of snapping. The rope grew hot, then ice cold, then scaly, like the back of a fish, then it reared up like a geyser, then burst into flames as it ripped through my grip tearing the remaining flesh from my palms. Backwards steps. Tiptoeing backwards as the other side began to fold. The heat destroying our pink faces. The sweat now pumping down backs and down chests. Screams from the crowd, entreaties to pull, pull, and pull. Don't give up. Just pull, pull, and pull. Silent agonized grunts. Then loud grunts and heavy whooshing of air into lungs. Tears of salty stinging light. Until total collapse. All at once. Completely spent. Looking up at a blue sky without so much as a single cloud. Begging for air to enter my lungs and screaming with pain throughout my whole body. The agony wracking my entire frame. Unable to move a muscle. Drenched in sweat. Panting. Lungs wheezing.

A shadow passed over, dropped a scrap of paper near my outstretched hand. A scribbled address and a time. I never did catch his name. I was added to the crew of a remodelling outfit that worked all over Manhattan. My duties included unloading and carrying sheets of sheetrock up and down stairwells, through buildings, and leaving them up against walls; unloading and carrying lengths of steel up and down stairwells, through buildings, and leaning them up against walls; carrying drills and saws from one place to another; getting in the way and being yelled at; cutting-up steel with a malfunctioning circular saw; grinding the rough edges off metal; watching the people who did the real work, do that work, in sweltering conditions, either underground, or in alleyways, or in penthouse apartments. Ten dollars an hour.

As I lay there on the grass, sucking in air, chest rising and falling, staring up into the blue sky—it made perfect sense that there should be no clouds to obscure the sun beating down—life was still all ahead of me, and I was as green as the scraggly grass beneath me.

A BEGINNERS GUIDE TO TAXIDERMY

'RECORD' button pressed on tape recorder.

Clears throat.

Chapter 1: Getting started. Very few hobbies can provide so much instant gratification for such a minimal investment as taxidermy. The primary consideration when commencing is finding a suitable place to do the work. Since a considerable amount of slimy viscera is inevitable, the location you select should be agreed upon in advance with other members of the household. Significant others will usually agree to some reasonable compromise when delicately approached, and indeed they generally turn out to be surprisingly enthusiastic when they see the end result. One cannot emphasize enough how much it pays off to have their consent upfront: especially if the project turns ugly, and involved, and the whole house begins to stink of badger entrails.

Coughs.

Locate the worktable or 'evisceration zone' in a well-lit place, near a clean water supply, if at all possible. There should be ample elbow room for eviscerating tools and sundry materials within easy reach. They should be laid out in a methodical manner so as to be instantly available. If say the muskrat you are working on gets agitated half-way through the process, you will want to get your hands on a scraper fairly quickly. A planning-ahead system is really the best way to gets things done. Neatness and order makes the whole thing so much easier. The kitchen table, the dining room table, or an infant's changing unit may prove suitable according to individual requirements.

Very often a combination of areas will be used. For example, skinning, fleshing, or squibbing operations might be done in the ensuite bathroom or downstairs toilet, while actual mounting work can be done in the family room, while the rest of your loved ones watch some light entertainment, such as a variety performance or nude dating contest. Tool requirements for taxidermy are few and simple; most of them can be fashioned from items lying around the house. For instance, a curved grapefruit knife with serrated edges is ideal for small mammals. When it comes to knives the first requisite is that they will slice nicely and easily through flesh; a surgeon's scalpel is ideal but refrain from bothering a physician—they may be purchased from a mail-order dealer for a nominal sum.

Clears throat noisily.

Learning by getting your hands dirty is much more than a well-worn cliché when it comes to taxidermy. However, knowing upfront a few of the accident black spots likely to be encountered in say, bird mounting will greatly help the amateur. Difficulties usually occur in skinning around the posterior or tail end...excuse me. Apologies, that damn television!

Faintly, from another room.

I asked you to turn it down! I'm recording the first chapter. At the door? Oh, just some idiot who wasn't happy with his dog. Gives him nightmares, apparently. What are you watching? This again. I suppose so. Pause it and I'll get the popcorn. The state of his calves. Why do they have so many tattoos on their legs these days? I don't get it. I mean you'd have to wear shorts all year round to get the milage out of them. Cup of tea? Fine, but don't go on any further on without me—I want to see who she picks. Let me just finish out the introduction to Chapter 1.

Clears throat noisily. Voice much clearer and louder now.

Where was I? Yes, here we go. Taxidermy is truly one of the greatest means of preserving nature that we still have at our disposal in the modern age. It can serve so many purposes quite aside from the obvious pleasure to be had in removing the insides of a creature and replacing with a mixture of polystyrene and borax: like for instance as an educational tool for children who will perhaps never meet a badger, a stoat, a pine marten, a fox—whilst stumbling or flailing through thick undergrowth; or to help struggling artists capture a truly life-like vivacity in their work; or just to sit up on top of the television set or in some nook in the house where it can accumulate dust and stare out blankly at the people watching a programme where the contestants have no clothes on.

Sound of doorbell ringing. Sound of footsteps. Door opening. Faintly.

What now? That's got nothing to do with me, sir. All I do is stuff them. What you do in the comfort of your own home is no...I will do no such thing! The process was explained to your daughter. She brought *Mr. Poppystockings,* I did the job, she was perfectly happy with the...Ah, would you ever head off with yourself! Oh really, what are you going to do about it? That's right—slink off with your tail between your legs.

Door slams. Sound of footsteps. Angry inflection to voice and very loud.

Let's start over again. Chapter 1: Getting started. Very few hobbies can provide so much instant gratification for such a minimal investment as...what's the point. Nothing is worth preserving. Our civilization is doomed. Everything is flying apart, and nothing remains to keep us together. Family means nothing. Religion means nothing. Taxidermy means nothing. Personally, I can't wait for the walls to come tumbling down around our ears. We thoroughly deserve it. A slow and steady decline towards a permanent extinction event once we've eradicated the planet of every other living creature. We are slowly building ourselves a zoo populated entirely by the human race and when you try and speak out...

Hi—yes, the tea, completely forgot all about it! No-no, I'll finish this later...it's fine.

'STOP' button pressed on tape recorder.

MOTORCYCLE MAN

In last night's dream my gaunt face superimposed itself on the mirrored visor of his motorcycle helmet. Despite his snakelike soothing noises and the calming gestures of his gloved hands, I arm myself with a rusty penknife. I will not go with him. My injuries, when dragged along the ground and forced onto his motorbike, are nothing compared to the moment when he slides back the visor and quells my protests with one well-timed Glasgow kiss. A brief interlude of happiness and relief, evident on the faces of my family when we're reunited. They embrace me joyfully, I feel their fingers digging into me, kneading the skin and bone I've been reduced to, then turning to express their deepest gratitude—discover their hero already trudging back to his idling chariot—concealed by a billowing cloud of blackest exhaust fumes.

The dream, and then this morning the phone call, which is in itself something to remark upon since nobody ever phones me anymore. The woman's voice sounded distraught. Motorcycle Man was lying comatose on her couch. His bike had spun out of control just outside Virginia town and he was thrown clean off. Skidded fifty feet along the hard shoulder before coming to rest on the side of the road, unable to move. This woman (Claire) then called an ambulance, travelled with him to the hospital, answered all the questions, and was witness to the moment when they tried to take off his helmet, his berserk trashing of the triage screens. The only sensible thing she could get out of him was a phone number.

He's in excruciating pain but she can't be sure of exactly what nature because he won't talk to her unless it's to ask her if I'm there yet.

My first reaction is a rapid onset of ice-cold reluctance to get involved. I'm an old man. I live with my daughter as a guest in her house. I'm like a fish that has hung around too long—I stink—and I can see it on the faces of the grandkids and that once obsequious son-in-law. They don't want me here. I know that. On the other hand, it's very comfortable in this room, I have my own television. I can watch whatever I want, whenever I want, so long as I keep the volume down low. On the cold winter nights I wonder what would have happened to me if I had stayed out there, sleeping rough, abusing myself the way I did for all those years; would I still be alive and if so just how pathetic and degrading would my existence have become were it not for the intervention of my friend and his chrome covered steed? He was the one that dragged me out of the gutter and brought me here. He saved my life.

I told the lady, in no uncertain terms, that Motorcycle Man was entirely her responsibility. As much as it pained me to say so, there was nothing I could do to help her. The phone returning arthritically to its cradle was a proper jab to the heart. I erupted into overflowing tears. I couldn't stop myself from blubbering, blubbering like a very tired old man. I wasn't crying for him (I thought); I was crying for myself. Here was the day. Here was the day of reckoning, and I was too weak, too pathetic, to do anything. I turned up the volume on my antiques show as high as it would go; I wiped the tears from my eyes with a pocket handkerchief and blew my nose; I considered the build-up of moisture on the bedroom window as a sign of how cold it was outside; I opened/closed my pocket-knife multiple times; and I did a thousand other inconsequential things before I finally called Claire back to beg for her forgiveness, explaining my initial reaction as mere shock, and offering her my full and undivided assistance.

Motorcycle Man refuses a proper name. It remains buried somewhere in the past. He has nothing by way of possessions, just his motorbike, the leathers on his back, the helmet on his head, and those two ancient monolithic motorcycle boots. They comprise his armour, as he careens along our motorways and back roads and dirt tracks to the wild primal roar of his antiquated mongrel machine (a composite of every bike conceived since the beginning of creation) as a modern-day knight errant. Always at breakneck speed, always pushing to the ultimate his ability to expect the unexpected. Does he have a buried death wish? I've often wondered about that. Is Motorcycle Man empty on the inside? Is there really a beating heart inside those tarnished leathers? All the myths and rumours that enshroud his stick-insect frame lend an air of dark menace, stories that engorge an already prurient desire for gossip about his origins, when nobody knows a thing about his backstory and never will.

It most certainly will not come from him, since he barely speaks a word, and when he does speak, listen very carefully because he only ever elucidates in a rasping whisper and never repeats himself. If you miss something he said, it's entirely your own fault. His motives and ideals are entirely his own and have never been adequately described or written down anywhere. All I can say with any degree of certainty is that his past, whoever he was before the helmet and bike no longer exists and that his conduct, and on what authority he acts has always remained shrouded in mystery.

"You're not going to Cavan!" screamed my daughter.

Arms crossed. A vein throbbing in the centre of her forehead. Of course, I could see her point of view. How responsible would it be to give money to an old man like me, an old man threatening to go half-way across the country, when undoubtedly he would end up in the nearest bar, piss it all away, and then slope back to the house with some cock and bull story about getting set-upon by teenagers! It was familiar territory for her. I had put her through so much already. Would it be likely that I would take off with no money in my pocket on a cold November night for a distant part of the country? Hardly. Therefore, my request for funding was emphatically denied. Regardless, I headed for the door with a shrug of shoulder and a bag of rags thrown over my back.

"If you leave this house don't think you can just..."

I walked for two miles and then slid down a steep grassy bank on my heels to the main road. My thumb pumped itself up, at the end of an outstretched and trembling arm. My first lift was with a lorry-driver who had to get out and help me climb up into the cab seeing as it was easily six feet up off the ground. A push to my bony backside and I was able to drag myself inside and close the door behind me. Once we got to rolling, he asked me my business and was tickled pink to hear me talk freely about my old friend, and how for once *he* needed *me*. It felt good to be treated like an adult for a change. To be given the respect of a listening ear and to smoke my first cigarette in many years. How long it had been since anyone had listened to me? And not with that distracted air, as if some wrinkled old piece of skin wrapped around a skeleton was moving its jaw up and down, like a turtle.

"Good for you, old timer!" the lorry-driver applauded my zest for life, the condescending cunt.

My second lift was with a middle-aged woman and her teenage son. She was eager to know what a man of my age was doing out so late at night. I didn't tell her much. She would have pulled over and insisted on calling my daughter. She reminded me a lot of my daughter, that same self-righteous tone, *it's for your own good!* to quieten my protests. I told her I was on my way to blessed adoration in the chapel. Every hour of every day required someone to be present with the host. She went out of her way to deliver me to the church, and from there I hitched a ride with a priest, and then a barman, after that a butcher's apprentice, a used car-salesman, a van load of stoned boys in a covers band whose name escapes me, and then a factory worker on the way home from a twelve-hour shift.

This puny old body and sparse grey hair no doubt helped ferry me from one side of the country to the other. A harmless old man. It took six hours without sleep, water, or food but I made it to the home of the woman I'd talked to on the phone. To Claire's house. Right to her doorstep; a modest house in a decent housing estate on the outskirts of the town. She answered the door to a stinking, weary, old man, and invited me, without a moment's hesitation inside her home. What struck me first was the lack of room in the hallway. I had to shimmy past piles of newspapers and disused furniture and black bin liners of unidentifiable 'stuff'. A hoarder. I ignored her offer of tea and the possible effects it would have on me to ask for directions to the injured party.

There he is, lying hunched-up on the couch, still in his leathers and with his helmet and visor pulled down to cover his eyes. The only concession he's made to being injured is to have removed his Motorcycle boots. They stand neatly to attention beside the couch. Neat beside each other and stinking to high heaven. The insides are like the rotting entrails of some roadkill so far gone with putrefaction that you cannot tell what animal it was to begin with. I have need to stagger backwards from the smell. As I do there's a bag of rubbish that gets kicked all over the floor and wakes him. He beckons me with a gloved hand to come close.

He needs to tell me something but there's no way of gathering what he's saying because his voice has dropped to no more than a faint sibilance. When I suggest taking off his helmet to hear him better, his entire body convulses. With some difficulty he pulls back his helmet, using both his hands, so that I can see his putrid mouth; at which point he begins to whine and whimper about not wanting to die.

"Cut that shit out!" I tell him.

It's behavior unworthy of a man of his stature. A man who's seen the kind of things he's seen. A man who has witnessed every kind of depravity and made it his business to clean up the mess. The stench of his whimpering acts like smelling salts. My tiredness and hunger slink away into the shadows of the room. Adrenaline seeps out of my pores. My silent fury prompts him to sit up in his sick bed, to hack up a large dollop of garish green phlegm. I've developed a crick in my neck from staring at him in this awkward position.

Claire describes where the bike is hidden (she pulled it off the road and covered it in a blanket) and informs me that we need to leave as soon as we are ready, which means now. Her partner is returning from the Middle East where he works in some capacity on the construction of tower blocks. No offence but we present an unusual sight: two withered old crones, one wearing a helmet and the other a wretched long face. She'll drive us to the place where the bike is concealed and after that we will have to look after ourselves. I watch her change Motorcycle

Man's incontinence nappy and clean his arse, while the tiny white skinned body writhes in agony, its withered penis ejecting a thin drizzle of dark orange piss into an old pot.

Soon I will be wholly responsible for the care of this defenceless mewling creature who still refuses to remove his motorcycle helmet. Soon he will be wholly dependent on me for his survival. With no time to think, Claire talks me through the activities I'll need to perform to keep his wound from becoming infected, hands me a plastic bag with all the medical items I'll need, and even offers me the lend of a wheelchair.

"Jesus, the time!" and she ferries her aged cargo in silence to the black spot on the road where the accident took place. She hands me a flashlight, wishes us luck, says her goodbyes in a faraway voice, and drives off.

I heave him across my back in a fireman's lift, his arms and legs dangling, and wonder at where this strength has come from.

Mechanically there's nothing wrong with the bike, and I get it started on a fourth attempt. Roaring into life it strains beneath me to gun straight out of there. I let it catapult the pair of us into the darkness. Motorcycle Man clings onto my back. He sways with the movement of the bike around every dip and turn of the road as I open her up. Two helmeted old men contorting the space between time and death; moving into the future. I begin to appreciate just how truly miserable I was in my daughter's prison room as we overtake a forty-foot articulated lorry and are lauded by its driver with an elephantine bellowing of its twin mounted trumpet air horn, lauded like the gods that we are on this darkest night of near zero visibility and constant searing sleet. A touch from Motorcycle Man on my shoulder alerts me to the exit he wants us to take, and I feel him move an envelope inside my jacket, deposited in the inside breast pocket.

After the slip road, we make the acquaintance of a deliciously desolate winding route through a cavalcade of darkly nodding trees. The bike slaloms through the gathering surface water when I hit a nasty pothole that sends us into a wearied sway, kicking Motorcycle Man off the back, sending him skidding across the road into a waterlogged ditch. I stop the bike with an inelegant skid and lumber through the darkness, armed with a flashlight, to fish his body out of the ditch. I wrench at his helmet with every ounce of my strength, but it will not detach from his head.

There! Off it comes and those baby blue eyes stare lifelessly at the trembling acolyte.

His faded leathers fit just fine. That is to say that they are skin-tight all over my body but that will change. I'll shrink to fit them. His boots too will fit me—I insist on that. It doesn't matter what size they are. I'll stretch them out to meet mine. To have stripped his body in such a manner and left his remains in a ditch might seem cold or indifferent but it's what he would have wanted; these fleshy appendages and sagging frames are nothing more than a transport mechanism—once the spirit has departed there is no other course of action but to pick the bones clean, to tear away the leather and let the creatures of the earth take away the flesh, as the microbial growth devours from inside out. Besides, he would also have known that I couldn't afford to bury him, having at my disposal no funds whatsoever.

A naked little body in tattered underwear sinking under brackish water.

Everything thus far feels like a dress rehearsal for this moment of coronation. The moment when I pull on his helmet and feel his fetid stench become my fetid stench. The visor through which I now view the world smears everything with a bleak streaky grey. The envelope and inside it a brief letter of instruction. His barely decipherable scribble describing the next case, their last known address, hair color, height, eyes, nickname; a very brief biography of a troubled teenager with head placed inside the jaws of temptation. And so now I assume those responsibilities, the awful burden, and of course the endless hardships that go hand in hand with this position, as none too subtle anxieties are ignited by the sound of my panicky breathing inside this oversized motorcycle helmet: *I want to go home... I need to lie down and rest... I can't do this...*

The leathers respond by constricting around my calves, thighs, across either gluteus maximus, all up along the back and shoulders and across the chest, to become as tight as a new layer of skin. The motorcycle boots fasten my feet tighter to the bike; and as if trying to fully focus my attention, the visor of the helmet turns opaque so that my field of vision is narrowed to a tiny corona, and with that a breathless whispering in my ear—I willingly submit to the strident instructions with screams muffled by the engine's roar—the chariot bearing me away from the white line and into the night sky.

PILLORIED

I wake up—or rather, regain consciousness—in a very odd body position. The shrill cry of a seagull returns me to my senses little by little, then all at once. Two bleary eyes blinking. Headache from hell. Sandpaper tongue. Here I am on a street-corner in some obscure part of the city early in the morning. A bolus of questions flowing towards me, clogging the inner workings of an already stressed system, while the broom that was propping up my backside falls away with a loud clatter to the paving stones. It would appear (and I still can't believe that I'm saying this) it would appear, that I am pilloried. I say that because my head and my hands are trapped between wooden boards. My body is at a right angle to my legs and my poor old arse is sticking out.

There's no conceivable way of removing either my head or my hands. I've pulled with all my might. No give whatsoever. It's like trying to remove a limb from its socket. And yet it's all that I can do for the longest time imaginable until goosebumps creep up along my exposed lower back. I can really feel the morning chill as shame continues to rush back inside of me from wherever it was parked up for the night. So now I'm cold, bothered, and trying to figure out just what the hell happened to get me here. Give it time. Chunks of the evening will return. Bits will congeal to dispel the darkness, heaved up from somewhere. As I wrack my brain to piece together exactly what happened, two rough palms cover my eyes, and I hear a heavy-chested cackle from behind as the owner of the hands asks me to guess who? It's an older woman's voice. When I refuse to offer her a suggestion, she shuffles over to one side.

"Ere a fag?" she inquires.

Her name is Nora. She has the face of a hobgoblin complete with wrinkles, warts, and whiskers. She roams the streets looking for drink, cigarettes, and anything else that's going. Before I have a chance to answer, she thrusts a hand into my shirt pocket, removes the squashed packet, takes one flattened cigarette for now and one for later, puts the packet back in my pocket, and then nods curtly to conclude our dealings. When I ask her for a favour, more of that cackling laughter erupts from a distressed set of lungs, more involuntary shaking, convulsions, a wave of her hand, as the cigarette dances luridly on her bottom lip.

"Not so friendly when you're sober," she croaks.

"Tell me. What did I do last night?"

She acts all shy and demure, so I'm perfectly aware of what she's getting at. I'm confident there is no way that anything happened between us. A fabrication. There is no possible way that I... but without contradictory evidence from my memories, I'm forced to take her at her word. My mouth is suddenly very dry. Rain drops form on the end of my long nose and drip like torture, just past the tip of my outstretched tongue. As much as I would like to free myself without creating a fuss or without bringing any additional disgrace and humiliation on myself, it will require someone to come along and open the lock that binds the upper and lower planks together.

Nora wanders away nursing her misconceptions. Presumably, I've been stuck here for the last five or six hours. I could die of exposure if someone doesn't help me out of this situation.

"Help! Help Me! Somebody Please Help Me!" I scream so loudly that it scalds the back of my throat.

I hear my voice echoing up and down the narrow street. It comes back sounding desperate and ridiculous, as if taunting me with its insincerity. I'm forced to take a break—there is nobody about at this hour of the morning—I should save my breath and wait until I see someone coming.

It's going to be alright.

I reassure myself. I tell myself lies. Someone is bound to help me. It's only a matter of time. A nice person will see my predicament and release me. They'll say something like "it's happened to the best of us" and will engineer a way of opening the pillory, and like a wild animal released from a trap I'll shoot off out of here and then...

Memories returning, with hunched up shoulders, kicking stones along the path at their feet, as if ashamed of themselves, unless...and it has to be considered a possibility, unless they are not real memories at all but remnants of dreams, dreams infused with alcohol. For I don't doubt that I was drinking and went too far on the rum—I'm quite certain on that score—but everything else is up for grabs, everything else is dawning on me with a creeping realization of my shameful situation here; pilloried in plain view of everyone passing me in the street as a consequence of my own behavior. Yet it seems unjustified that I should be held accountable for the actions of a drunken fool now that I'm sober again. The problem is that I can't say either way if my position here is justified: I simply don't know.

Wait, I hear voices coming towards me! I hear loud vulgar conversations. Merrymakers coming back from a party somewhere within the city walls. A gang of young people still enjoying themselves from the night before. They are re-living the best moments by re-enacting them in silly voices full of spite and hatred. I was like them once; look at me now. I really am a disgrace to my family and to myself. I'm a terrible person, a disgusting piece of trash. My self-worth has slumped to the level of spill-over from a metal bin on the city street. Of course, they won't help me. Instead they remove my shoes and socks and start tickling the soles of my feet with a feather.

"Stop that! Help me out of here, please!" I scream between bouts of excruciating tickling. Their attitude awakens the beast in me. Their inability to recognize a fellow human being. Their lack of empathy. How would they feel, if they were the one in stocks on a wet, cold, foggy morning? From behind me one member of the gang places a crown on my head— a cheap cardboard replica from a fast-food outlet. They find it amusing that I swipe it off, break down in tears, beseech them for some common decency in my hour of need. They continue to tease me while I weep and shout for help. They try to provoke me with insults, until finally, finally they grow bored of my weeping and the watery snot hanging out of my nose, and they return wordlessly to their early morning journey.

I have no work. I'm completely broke. I survive by begging and playing the recorder to elicit pity. I came with the ambition to find a place on one of the many merchant galleys leaving for Spain and Portugal and France, but not one of them would give me a start. When forced to concede that I had never been to sea before nor even set foot on a boat, not one of them would give me the chance to prove myself. The bastards laughed in my face when I explained that it had been my dream from childhood to sail away to some foreign land. When I explained that I was a farm labourer from the midlands, that I was sick to death of crippling myself for a pittance from miserly farmers, why, these men laughed even harder at me! Did it make me sound work-shy to state plainly and honestly my distaste for back-breaking farm work? Or was it my cherished dream that was so pitiful to these seasoned seamen? Either way, something about the way in which I spoke amused them so much that they could not help but laugh in my face and ridicule my accent. All except one. And he was a man that I met by chance in a tavern, captain of *The Pissant,* who offered me a berth without asking even the most cursory details about my life or experience. He liked the cut of my jib, and he could tell a good one when he saw it, or so he said.

Captain O'Malley asked me there and then to join him on an epic and dangerous journey into unchartered waters where he confidently predicted that we would recover a horde of gold doubloons buried in the hull of an Armada schooner still perched on top of an underwater shelf out there in the Atlantic. The light danced with mischief in his eyes and there was a scent of danger from his person. Answer quick: Would I join him on his mad voyage? The promise was a share in the booty and a share in the glory. When I pointed out that it all sounded too good to be true, he grabbed hold of my elbow and dragged me onto the nearest 30-footer, where I was shown what would be my very own perfectly fitted-out cabin. No sign of bedbugs or buggery. In case I asked around, it was true that he did not own the ship, yet, but there were a number of investors involved who were waiting on payouts and then...

His vim and vigour were irrepressible. I wanted so desperately to believe what he was saying because I could see how desperately he wanted to believe it for himself. I wanted to agree because it was exactly what I had dreamed of as a child picking potatoes out of frozen soil, heaving hay around a field with a pitchfork, avoiding the precise backward kick of a mean-spirited cow. My heart leapt with excitement at the thought of our slow, stately movement past the other ships and into Galway Bay. I learn fast, that's the thing about me. I only need to be told once, and then I can do it for myself without further instruction. I didn't want to be taken out of school and loaned out to every farmer in the parish looking for a pair of hands and a young back. But that was my lot. I was the ignorant boy of ignorant parents to be paid a pittance and then given dog's abuse for it. I'd run away to find excitement and adventure in this town. With every rejection my mood sunk lower until it made sense to stay in the tavern out of the cold and listen to the strange stories and songs sung in a tongue I could not understand.

It was while contemplating my lowly retreat back to the midlands with my tail between my legs that I'd met Captain O'Malley. He spoke so movingly and so convincingly of *The Pissant* that I forgot my worries and vowed to help him set sail laden with goods and manned with the finest seamen. O Captain, why did you see the need to tell such seductive tales to an ignorant fool like me?

It was while I collected the names and fares of the other young recruits that he disappeared into a foam of apathy—I searched for him everywhere, lugging the sack of coins with me up and down the quays—until I too lost faith and took to drinking myself into oblivion with money that did not belong to me like a right cretin so that it was inevitable that I'd fall foul of the law at some stage.

As for now, there is a sense of urgency. With the rising of the sun, the purification of these seedy streets aglow in orange hues, windows reflecting the flames of some silent fire rippling through the buildings, while I try to illuminate the darkness inside of my head. I begin to perceive the outline of some fuzzy recollections and cringe away from them. I'm returning to myself, slowly and unsurely, remembering that I have so much to be thankful for: my health for instance, apart from my creaking knees, wheezing lungs, rotten teeth, receding gums, receding hairline, blurred vision, slipped discs, hammer toes, lumbago, hearing loss, fungal infections...

"There he is!"

A woman and her children come towards me. They stop short of embracing me. She will surely tell me what I did last night when she finishes her conversation with the man in the navy-blue uniform and peaked cap. She will give it to me straight. I'm a little apprehensive to tell the truth. Not only is she refusing to make eye contact, but it's clear to me that her measured tone and serenity is for the benefit of the man in blue. Her just-wait-until-I-get-you-home face appears for a split-second when he goes back to his notepad to flick away a ladybird and get the spelling of my name right. A glimpse of the future state is that I will have to apologize and scrape; wear a sack cloth; eat cinders; crawl on my belly; avert my eyes; shed a few tears; have a mini breakdown; grope for forgiveness; endure silences; start some kind of counselling; and that will only be the start of it.

The poor kids are bored and restless; the youngest is clutching his pee-pee through his shorts and dancing from one leg to the other. I'd love to remember what their names are, but it will mean consigning Captain O'Malley and *The Pissant* and those wonderfully picaresque vignettes to the scrap yard of my soul. Yes, it's all coming back to me now—how sad—I live a comfortable middle-class existence in a housing estate full of complete strangers and last night was about team building and ensuring our sales targets for the year are not only met but exceeded. The other office staff in the recruitment firm where I work will be absolutely thrilled when they hear about what I got up to on a company night out and how my wife (whose name escapes me for the moment) had to come and rescue me.

"Daddy why are you dressed like a pirate?" asks the older child.

A police car swerves onto the street. Two men step out: a tall police officer and a priest in his collar. The police officer points him in my direction and as the priest approaches he fishes out a set of keys attached to a long piece of wood. I get the impression that they are going to release me until he slips them discreetly back into the pocket of his cassock, and they join with the woman and first police officer just out of earshot.

The woman glances over with a troubled look on her face. The priest removes his glasses to wipe the tiredness from his eyes. The police officers compare identical small notebooks where the pages are being flicked backwards and forwards with an eerie synchronicity.

I turn my attention to the children who continue to stare at me with wonder, concern, and even perhaps pity, on their sweet little faces. The older one repeats her question and stamps her foot when I fail to answer. This is clearly not ideal in terms of our relationship. In years to come, they may well remember this moment and wonder if this was where their problems originated, seeing their father in a pillory, dressed as a pirate, still a little worse for wear from the night before. The youngest is still clutching at himself, knocked-kneed and with a look of fright written all over his features.

"Captain O'Malley, stop that! It's called a pillory. Daddy has been pilloried."

"I'm not Cat-in Malley," says the youngest, a tear wavering in his eye "I'm Daniel!"

LIE DOWN PLEASE

You were warned over the phone. Please don't be late, they said. Please make sure you give yourself plenty of time for your appointment, they said. It was reiterated and reemphasized, and you got the message loud and clear. A text message received the day before the consultation reminded you again not to be late and warned you that if you were late the consultant would be forced to rush the procedure which could possibly result in a less than desirable outcome. Not only were you late, how late being irrelevant, but the secretary has to confirm all your details before you can go in to see him. The secretary is seated low down behind a computer screen, which explains the blue sheen on her glasses. She has a mask over her face so you can't see her mouth. You can see that her hair is not only thinning towards the back of her skull but also that she has styled it in a way that only draws attention to it.

You can't stop yourself from nodding off. A narcoleptic tendency with origins unknown. That is to say one day you started to feel tired in work and despite the coffee and shedding of clothes, you face-planted onto your keyboard and sent the mouse spinning across the office floor. You simply can't stop yourself from abruptly falling asleep, and it's been going on like this for months. The other doctors have found nothing wrong with you. Are you sleeping at night? Yes, eight hours, ten hours, twelve hours, but you're still tired all the time. Why is that? Emotional problems? Stress at work? Relationship issues? There's no simple explanation for it, and the prescribed drugs haven't made a blind bit of difference. Maybe there is nothing wrong with you at all, and this is all in your head. Has that occurred to you?

You have come to see the pre-eminent expert in this country who deals specifically with conditions of this kind. You are at your wits end. Your face is bleak and broken with the pale marks of exhaustion under your eyes. You have two small children; you are very happily married. You are extremely happy in the job you have at present. Couldn't be happier. Is there something in your relationship that has recently changed? Is there something that's causing you to worry? Has there been a bereavement recently? Do you find yourself getting stressed out about things in general? Would you describe yourself as a happy person? On a scale from one to ten with one being miserable and ten being…

A full battery of blood tests have revealed nothing. They can't find a single thing wrong with you. Your urine doesn't show anything unusual. Must be all in your head. The thing is you know that there has to be something wrong with you because you just don't feel *yourself*. Worse than feeling *unwell* in a general sense, and not feeling *yourself* specifically, as you drove from work to your mother in law's house where the kids are being minded—you woke-up—just as your car burst through a ditch and into a meadow. You had very nearly killed a woman off her bike as well as yourself.

The consultant is extremely put out by the fact you're late. He's the punctilious type. You can tell from every detail in his office and the way his staff act. The receptionist for instance seemed nervous as she typed your details into her system; the nurse who called you in from the waiting room was visibly shaking. The consultant bristles his elaborate eyebrows against perched spectacles to look you up and down. Mollified by your appearance, he expects a very detailed explanation for your lateness. You tell him there was a really bad road accident, the cars were backed up, there was no way around—you apologise profusely for the inconvenience, and you thank him again and again, for seeing you at such short notice, even though you've actually waited three months to get an appointment with him.

Those two angry caterpillars hovering above his watery blue eyes are sated, at least for the time being, when you fill him on all the gory details from the accident you passed: the crumpled cars, the shoes on the road, those tiny little cubes of tempered glass rolling in waves. You'll just feel a little pinch. Nothing to worry about. Except you are more worried now than at any other time in your life. A very large needle is inserted into your upper gum with agonising slowness. Your entire mouth becomes swollen. Your tongue becomes a large unwieldy lump of gagging material that you are afraid of biting into by accident because you feel no pain whatsoever. The nurse takes photographs of the inside of your mouth. You are forced to mumble and groan because you can no longer speak. The power of speech has been removed by his injection. When he explains what he's doing and asks you questions all you can do is grunt through your nose and nod your head.

The consultant exhales noisily when he consults the developed photographs and shrugs his shoulders before shoving his entire hand inside your mouth. When you feel his fingers around your epiglottis, you begin to gag. He becomes infuriated and removes his hand with an audible sigh of frustration. First you were late, and now this. He insists that he will need to strap you down to the bed, and the nurse has to assist him in making sure that the leather straps are firmly positioned across your legs and abdomen pinning your arms down by your sides. You are already whimpering and growing uneasy as he has decided on a course of treatment without giving you any of the options. He has made the decision on your behalf, for you.

For the last minute or so, his nurse has been trying to get his attention by saying Dr. X, sir, Dr. X, sir, Dr. X…He places his forceps delicately on a metallic tray with a tinny clatter and turns on his nurse. If she would rather be somewhere else that is entirely fine with him, because he doesn't need her anymore. She reminds him, in a tremulous voice, that she has to go to the crèche to pick up her little ones. He doesn't give a damn about her little ones, but he nods his head and says, of course if you have to go then by all means, but tomorrow they will have to sit down and have a little chat about how things are going.

So things are obviously not going so well. His nurse apologizes to you by a slight nod and flickering of eyes above the mask. She is genuinely unhappy to have to leave you alone with him and knows that she really shouldn't do this, but her hands are tied, and maybe this situation would never have happened, and he wouldn't be so pissed off—if you'd managed to get there on time.

He waits until he's sure the nurse is gone and then quickly shoves his entire arm down your throat in one violent movement. You saw him put on a long glove made from clear blue plastic. Over the crinkly surface of this glove he'd rubbed a lubricant squeezed from a tube, and you watched him lather it up into a white sticky foam, but you never for one instant considered the idea of his putting his entire arm right down your throat. There wasn't an opportunity to flinch or to stop him from reaching deep inside your body, and now he has, so don't even think about closing your mouth.

His hand, once it goes past your throat, sinks deeper and deeper into your body. What exactly he is he hoping to locate? There's no point in searching his face for an answer because it's a cloud of blank savage authority. This is the thing he is doing to you because it is his will to do it to you. You came to this place of your own free will. You can have no complaint to make now that he has his arm rammed all the way down your throat up to his elbow. The worst part is that he is rushing now to get to the root of the problem; he's really searching with an open palm, feeling along each plane and seam of sticky viscera for the obscure thing that he's looking for but can't quite put his finger on. There is no pain involved:

you're so numbed you cannot feel a thing.

The consultant is muttering angrily about something but has reached such a nadir of agonised pleasure that he cannot possibly stop himself from emitting a strangulated groan. At the inquest, he will certainly arrive on time and with the same serious face that he always wears. They will talk about his impeccable record and the fact that he has never been in any kind of trouble before. That nobody ever raised concerns about him until now. His twenty-five years of service to the community and the continued love and respect of his peers will exonerate him. He will no doubt claim that you came into his room and opened your mouth as wide as you could so that as he examined the inside of your mouth you swallowed down on his arm and forced it to go deeper and deeper inside until he was worried for his own safety and wellbeing.

Also that you were late for the consultation.

The inquest will undoubtedly find him innocent of all charges made against him and will find against you for bringing charges of defamation without just cause. You will be forced to pay for the costs incurred by the court system; also you will be expected to pay your solicitor the fee that was never agreed up front since he was privately convinced that you would not win the case and is therefore demanding a flat fee that is not dependent on the outcome. The nurse will say that she was not in the room at the time and that she had never witnessed him misbehaving with anyone's insides before the alleged incident or since. Her shaky voice and white-as-a-sheet complexion will be put down to nerves, a fear of public speaking. Afterwards you will be left standing on your own on the steps of the courthouse without a friend in the world.

With all that in mind, it makes complete sense to bite down hard on his arm. The restraining strap around your jawline is only made of plastic and is quite easily freed from by a tilt of the head and a dip of your neck underneath the stirrup. Next you must gaze up into his eyes and cough so that you distract his attention. There he is, looking at you to see what is happening as you quickly engulf and suck him further inside. That's right, a deep breath, and he starts to disappear altogether. Head-first of course so that his screams are muffled inside your trunk and his torso is pulled deeper and deeper inside your body with the peristaltic movements of your neck muscles and your abdominal muscles and your pelvic muscles so that the restraints are pushed past the point of bursting and pop open, one by one, with the angriest of sounds.

Now that he is almost fully inside you, there is the small matter of his kicking legs which are a real nuisance. Then of course you see how dirty the soles of his shoes are—so you manipulate them off by undoing the laces with your tongue, which takes ages because of the numbness. Now he has disappeared entirely inside your body. You feel him moving around in there. It must be a pen in his breast-pocket that is causing that sharp pain in your abdomen. But that will be passed out of you soon enough. He is fighting his way inside of you like a coiled up little beast. It must be strange going back inside after such a long absence. But we all know it's never a good idea to go back to somewhere that you left in a hurry and with misgivings—it will never be the same when you go back there. Everybody knows that, but nobody ever talks about it.

You stand up tall after the procedure, and it feels awkward to move when you have such a heavy load inside you. You have to waddle over and back just to retrieve your coat from the stand in the corner of the room. It really is a man's world, you think, as you sway across the room, smashing the framed doctorates and family photographs adorning every piece of free wall space in this poky, overwarm consulting room. He won't stop thrashing around inside you, despite the beatings you administer. He won't stop struggling to get back out, so that he can abuse the next patient.

The problems won't stop here, either. Now you will have to take the boat over to England for a procedure because nobody in this backward country will allow it to be conducted here. It will be a long journey over and then a shameful wait in some other dingy office and then a protracted procedure to get this thing out of your body. You just want to get it out before people in work notice. There is a phone on his desk, so why not just ring them from here and get it over with? The other practicalities include a place to stay for the night over there and should you fly or get the boat?

In the reception area you encounter the nurse who has returned with her children. She is stricken with guilt and why shouldn't she be? You brush past her and ignore the faces of her two adorable children. She knew what was going to happen to you, and she did nothing about it. But she came back after the fact because she thought she could be of some assistance in helping you to deal with the aftershock. See he's been doing this for years and to so many women, but nobody has ever wanted to speak out. Fine, then she can give you a lift to the train station and you can begin the long journey to have this monster aborted. To make things easier for you the nurse buys you magazines for the journey, to take your mind off things.

The rest of the time is spent waiting. Waiting for the opportunity to board the plane. Waiting for the train to arrive at the platform. Waiting on the train for the journey to the clinic. Waiting in the waiting room of the clinic. It's a good thing you brought all those magazines with you. There are other people in the waiting room. They don't want to make eye contact with you either. They would rather drop dead than be recognized. They would rather run a mile than talk to you or anyone else. The waiting room is so stacked with magazines that you can't possibly imagine a world without magazines. It would be unthinkable. Your name is called by a head that sticks into the room and instantly retracts. They are so nice that it makes you want to puke. They make you suspicious by their niceness, and when she asks if you were able to sleep last night you confirm that you slept like a baby. Maybe that wasn't the right thing to say.

The whole business is over in less than an hour. When they are done you are helped back to your feet by really friendly staff, and it feels just fine. Everything feels just fine. They ask you how you feel, and you say that you feel fine. Perfectly fine, but almost immediately there is the return of that protracted yawn. You could fall asleep standing up. Having the consultant inside you was great in terms of the narcolepsy, but now that he has been removed you're back to square one. The next thing you feel a bit woozy. You take a tumble that brings all the tools they used down with you. There on the floor of the room you meet the acquaintance of other life forms, microscopic, invisible to the naked eye, no matter what happens next, just remember one thing: this is all your fault.

CEREMONY

It took many weeks to finally convince my wife that we really ought to attend the ceremony, that it was our responsibility, morally speaking, to attend the ceremony, that to avoid doing so would be to finally admit defeat after such a long and heroic display of stoicism by the local community. So certain was I, so utterly convinced, that I didn't even give it much thought—the actual real-life event—until the night before the ceremony was due to take place. The night before, I discovered that my confidence lacked foundation, had all been wafer-thin bravado, layered on top of brittle positivity, layered on top of an abstract notion that things would somehow work out for the best of their own accord.

The mental image I had on the morning of the ceremony—of a huge crowd viewed from above, moving as one great amorphous mass of stinking arms and legs through the just recently opened iron gates, across the flattened-down grass, and around the huge craters of brackish water and slippery mud—made me feel uneasy and reluctant to budge from the embrace of our comfortable leather couch. When the time came to pack up all the items we would need and to get into the car, I hesitated. All that big-boy-bluster had been nothing more than a facade to hide behind; on the inside I was a scared little man with no certainties to cling to and no figure of authority to place my trust in.

Broadly speaking, the concept of the ceremony, organized by the City Council in conjunction with the International Arts Festival committee, was to bear witness and celebrate the casting-off of all the misgivings the general public harboured about hosting an event of this magnitude, so near to the official end, when dissenters were still nervous about crowds and the possibility of some new previously unidentified risk. Despite the horrific weather forecasted and the prevailing cynicism in the media and online, we were going to make our presence felt, to hail a glorious coming together of so many things: a festival of international artists and performers finally emerging after so many years of exile from the chrysalis of imposed isolation, to show our support for an industry that had been decimated in recent times by wave after wave of sanctions and cancellations and endless postponements.

After a tense hour-and-a-half of petty squabbling, we found a suitable place to leave the car, thankful that our arguing had not woken the infant in his car seat. At which point I asked my wife if maybe we were being irresponsible and should we just turn around and go back home again? So convinced was she that I was being facetious, she didn't break stride or stop to seriously consider what I'd just said. Instead, she began to remove the changing bag, the extra nappies, his booties, his zip-up romper suit, his drinks tray, his strap-on carrier device that would need to be disentangled to fit him into. Perhaps she was so tired that she had not properly heard what I'd said. I repeated myself. Ha-Ha-Ha, she replied, in a flat monotone and continued with the painstaking process involved in doing anything at all with a small baby.

It felt like we had no sooner stepped away from the car than a huge crowd swept us along like silt in a fast-flowing river with me transporting our newborn in the strap-on baby carrier across my chest and my wife pushing the buggy laden with his items. People were coming at us from all angles. Smiling, unthinking people, some of whom reached out to touch the baby with their cold-sore lips and unclean hands, to make physical contact with the innocence and perfect beauty of a newborn, despite my repeated warnings to stay well back. The newborn had to be admired, fondled, touched, grabbed, coddled, smothered by strangers who felt the right to do so when a baby was present: forgetting not only their manners but the advice of our medical practitioners. I didn't want to seem rude, but in the end I was forced to repel these well-wishers crowding our personal space by striking out at them, albeit lightly, with a miniature parasol stripped from the side of the buggy.

You might need to change his nappy, they said. He looks hungry, poor soul, feed him, said others. When he cried out in fear with real tears bursting from his frightened eyes, they declared that he was tired. See, when a baby is tired that's when they act unattractive to others and so there must be an excuse. Tiredness is the tried and trusted apologia, but really he was scared shitless by all the strange faces looming over him. I reassured the little mite by jigging his little hands up and down as if he were dancing to a tune. Not only was I attempting to reassure him, but myself. Something was rippling through the crowd. A feeling of unease firstly, and then a palpable concern—unhappy faces, angry faces, a distant far-away look in their eyes, these people were frightened and spooked.

They were attempting to escape back out of the gates through which we had all recently passed. My wife and I agreed, without either of us uttering a word, the best course of action was to simply return to our car and go home. This was certainly no place for an infant. Too many people crammed into this restricted space, which was limited by the fact that the site for the ceremony was on a peninsula. A massive mistake had been made by the organizers and with nobody visible to marshal or control the movement of the crowd—the situation was quickly becoming overwhelming.

In the background, we could hear distant thudding music from enormous stacks of speakers and the voice of a woman through the PA instructed us all to stop pushing, or the ceremony would be called off entirely. This served only to properly mobilize a fresh stampede of people coming the opposite direction to us, and then screaming and shouting as other people pushed back against them. With the baby in our midst we expected people to back away, to try to go around, rather than straight through us, but they just kept coming in wave after wave. It wasn't them that were doing the pushing; the heave was coming from miles away in the crowd, and the ripple effect was a potential endangerment of our infant son's life.

My wife quite understandably began scream at the people coming straight at us, to watch out where they were going. I tried to stay connected to her, but the crowd broke the grip between our hands. We were separated. She had the buggy with all of his items while he remained stuck to my chest. I called my wife's name and implored the people all around me to let me through. It was vital that I stay connected to her. It was vital that we stay together for the sake of our little one. She had everything we needed to keep him content: his rattle, his bottle of juice, his porridge, his nappies, his wipes, his cuddly toys, his thermometer, his extra hats, all of his extra clothing—she had everything!

I called out her name above the milling crowd of strangers pushing me backwards, then pushing my sideways, then pushing me forwards—all the time with my arms locked in front of my chest to protect the infant and begging the people around me to mind the baby. But the people around me were scared for themselves and their families and had lost their heads in the panic. It was everyone for themselves; they couldn't help it if they were being pushed into me. But they refused to acknowledge the fact or make eye contact when I screamed at them. The situation was deteriorating at an alarming rate.

Next thing I know, I'm face to face with a man I'd served many years ago when I worked in a corner shop. It was slightly awkward seeing him again because we hadn't set eyes on each other in donkeys' years and the last time we had seen each other was in a confrontational scenario. Now he refuses to acknowledge me, despite the glint in his eye. He knows exactly who it is in front of him but pretends to be just another stranger. He pushes past me so aggressively that other people in my vicinity grab him by the shirt and pull at his hair. I try to think of an intelligent, conciliatory, or even witty opening remark, but though I try and try to think of something, anything, to say to him, all I can do is give him an apologetic little smile.

You know, you don't have to work here, if you don't want to!

My attitude to the work was what had upset him as I scanned the items from his basket and lumped them into a plastic bag. He took exception to the fact that I was visibly disinterested and would not affect a happy disposition while serving him, that I should be privately fuming at having to work in a corner shop three nights a week to pay the rent on a cold, damp bedsit, and to buy the cheapest cans of beans, briquettes, breakfast cereals, milk, and all the other essentials whilst simulating an interest in my poorly chosen college course. If I was going to have a pissy attitude, then he should be served by someone else.

I'd snapped at him. It was wrong of me, and I knew it then, too. I should never have told him to f-off. Even if it was mostly muttered under my breath. Incensed by my response to his perfectly reasonable observation, this customer had demanded to see the manager. He wanted an apology first but maybe even that wouldn't be enough to settle the matter to his satisfaction. He stood to one side of the long queue of people I was forced to continue serving while the manager was being sent for. There was no manager in the shop at the time, so I improvised and had another cashier pretend to be the manager and listen to his complaint. Without receiving a full apology or even an admission of guilt the man stormed out of the shop pumped-up with outrage and bluster. I ignored his dagger-like stares and continued to serve the endless line of banal customers and their banal requirements: toilet paper, cigarettes, magazines, sandwiches, lottery tickets, chewing gum, pencils, bars of chocolate, washing powder, sanitary towels, condoms, phone credit, bus tickets, custard, lubricant, elastic bands, blades, batteries AA and AAA, crisps, fizzy drinks, bottled water, ice cream cones...

My wife appeared gasping for air and grabbed hold of my coat-sleeve. She was screaming at me to get a good firm grip and to pull her out of the crowd. She was drowning in a sea of nostrils, curly hair, damp jackets, earrings, beards, lipstick, bad breath, runny eyes, woolly hats, sharply fingered nails, wailing children, red-faced pensioners. The people around her were working in unison to force her into the nearest eddy of swirling bodies and gibbering faces, working in unison to try to knock her onto the ground so that she would be trampled into submission by feet that did not care enough to try and rescue her. She was screaming my name and reaching for me. I grabbed her by both arms and pulled her towards me.

...thought I'd never see you again, she said. Her eyes were filled with tears. She looked into the face of our son and pressed a hand against his cheek. How long had he been crying? She was asking me a question, but I wanted to tell her about the man I'd seen just a few moments earlier. I wanted to tell her the story about him and about working in the shop. I started, but I could tell that she wasn't interested in listening to this story. Instead she was annoyed at me for bringing up something so ridiculously inconsequential at this unprecedented moment in our lives—she might well have been dragged away and God forbid what might have happened to her.

It was a miracle that we had been reunited. That our little boy was unharmed. That we were all together in the middle of these crazy horrible people that were all thrashing around us hysterical with panic, when if we all just stayed perfectly still and waited for things to calm down...

My wife was then torn away from me again. Or, rather, the crowd around me had decided to go in one direction, taking me and our infant son in one direction, while the crowd around my wife had decided to go in the opposite direction and our hands were torn from each other, despite the best efforts of both of us to stay linked. She's screaming and I'm screaming and we're trying to get back to each other, but the fact is that we're crammed so tightly into these eddying subcrowds within the larger overall sea that it's impossible for an individual to go in the direction that they want to. Instead you are carried along despite the tears and tantrums of the little one strapped to your chest. He wants his mammy, and you, you want your wife.

It couldn't be. It's simply not possible—that was in another time and place a lifetime ago. I could hear the song playing in the nightclub with all the tacky associations, and there she is just standing on the edge of the dance floor with her hands in her pockets. It's the same girl now matured into a middle-aged woman in glasses with her hair done differently and of course the look of abject fear in her eyes, but it's undoubtedly the same person that I shared my first kiss with. I never even knew her name. I had been determined to get it over with—to experience what all the others had done many times—I had vowed to myself to get my first 'shift' with whoever happened to be standing there.

She was standing there with her hands in her pockets. She didn't suspect a thing, and when I asked her out to dance she made a vague gesture of assent. We held each other in a stranglehold and swayed from one foot to the other; then instinctively our mouths locked into place and this stranger's large full tongue is rotating slowly around the inside of my mouth in a steady examination of every part therein, while my own tongue is sparked into a similar mode of action, and the two large hard muscular tongues grind against each other in one continuous deadly struggle that feels like a tense, wrestling manoeuvre.

This endless shift continues right through the remainder of the first song and through the next two songs with our bodies still swaying and her head thrown back so that her whole gob is wide open. All the while I'm asking myself if I'm doing it right or should I be taking a break every so often? It doesn't seem like I should. She has not detached herself or tapped out and so we continue to battle tongues with gusto until the tempo of the music changes and there are more people dancing around again. She disengages with a smile and a long wipe of her mouth along the back of her hand.

I try to think of an intelligent, conciliatory, or even witty opening remark, but though I try and try to think of something to say to this woman from my past, all I can do is give her a thumbs up and an apologetic little smile. She is perfectly clear about considering me a stranger and smiles wanly not at me, but at the little person strapped to my chest. I might have done more to help her, but I was too busy shouting for my wife and hoping that this insanity would somehow resolve itself by peaceful means. Yes, I really should have done more to help her when she was knocked to the ground and trampled over, but I just assumed someone else would do something, risking their life for hers. Plus I had the infant to think about.

Being jostled by a big heavy-set man brings me back to my senses and then this old dear starts to pester me for something. She's telling me something that isn't quite registering until she gives me a hard slap across the backside and pulls my arm to go with her through the crowd. Of course, I try to break free from her hold, and it occurs to me at the same time that I haven't checked on the child strapped to my chest in ages—which is the point at which I realize I am in a harness of some description and that the old dear is using it to prevent me from escaping her clutches. She shoves a bottle of watered-down milk into my mouth and attempts to pull down my pants in front of everyone milling around us. I kick and struggle so much that I manage to get away from her, to merge back in with the crowd. I hear her calling my name, but I don't care if I never see her again.

After that, I got really tired of pushing through the crowd. I got so tired that I felt like dropping to the ground, but I knew that if I allowed that to happen I would be trampled to death like the poor woman I'd shared my first kiss with. I didn't want that to happen to me, to be trampled by all those impersonal feet and shoes and boots—that didn't appeal to me at all. Not only was I tired but I had these mysterious pains—one in my left knee and one in my lower back—and I couldn't seem to do anything to rid myself of them—they were just constant and dull and irritating in the extreme.

Not only that, but I felt that the people around me were suddenly less patient with me and the speed of my movements. They kept groaning and muttering every time they tried to get around me, for whatever reason, they kept shoving me out of the way. Then this beautiful young woman with a compassionate face approached and took the baby away with her, ripped him clean out of my hands. She said I was aging quite badly and needed to go into a home where I would receive the kind of around-the-clock care I so desperately needed. All of this came as quite a shock, and I didn't agree with anything she was telling me in that moment. On the other hand, I did quite fancy the idea of a long rest and someone else going to the trouble of feeding me and washing me and putting me to bed.

The next thing you know, I'm practically face to face with one of my oldest friends in the world. God, the japes we got up to. The fun we had and the holidays and the carousing and the laughter and the days at matches watching teams play each other and beat the daylights out of each other and then onto the pub afterwards for pints and whiskies and the mighty chats and the shared miseries. So many memories, Lord bless us and save us, they were some mighty times back then, really and truly.

I try to think of an intelligent, conciliatory, or even witty opening remark, but though I try and try to think of something to say to this great friend from my past, all I can do is give him a thumbs up and an apologetic little smile. I even remember his name and I say it to him as he's being dragged past me, but he doesn't want to acknowledge me. It's a grudgeful manner in which his head turns as we slide past each other, making eye contact and to say hello, but nothing more than that. Hello, was all he was willing to say and even that was, like I said—said grudgingly—as if it had put him out, to say hello, when he could have at least asked about my family or how my wife was doing...

By this stage, I was willing to admit that I was sad to be alone in the crowd and that I missed my wife and my infant son. They had been gone for hours, and there was no denying that I wanted to see them again. I wasn't sure if it would be possible to go home, but I did want to see them again, even if it was just a fleeting glance. With that in mind, I grew emboldened and fought my way through the crowd in every direction and pushed people onto the ground, trampled over anyone who happened to be beneath my feet without even looking down. I shouted their names and cried my heart out. It was no good. Nothing would bring them back.

Then I was forced, by a great bulge of backwards moving people, to clamber over a low wall, behind which was a pile of builders' gravel. The people standing up there had a slightly better view, so I fought my way to the top of the gravel pile. I could see all the heads bobbing, all those haircut styles, the different colours, the differently colored hats that many people were wearing, and even the kinds of jackets and coats they had on. The expressions on the faces—I could see them too: anger and frustration and dismay and horror and disbelief but mostly just no expression at all. When I started to shout at these people from my position at the top of the mound, when I tried to explain to them that we could get out of here alive by just standing still, even for an hour—that it would all end much sooner and with fewer casualties—not a single person in the crowd paid any attention.

That is why I skidded all the way back down the pile and rejoined the crowd. I had to pretend to be one of them. I had to act like I was just as scared and unhappy as them. That I felt exactly the same way as them. Which I did, so there was really no reason to pretend in the first place. But even knowing all that didn't stop me from pretending. I don't know why. It seemed easier, somehow, to pretend.

ABOUT THE AUTHOR

Brian Coughlan lives in Galway City, Ireland. His first collection of short stories *Wattle & daub* was published by Etruscan Press in 2018 and was a Foreword Indies Finalist that year.

Books from Etruscan Press

Zarathustra Must Die | Dorian Alexander
The Disappearance of Seth | Kazim Ali
The Last Orgasm | Nin Andrews
Drift Ice | Jennifer Atkinson
Crow Man | Tom Bailey
Coronology | Claire Bateman
Viscera | Felice Belle
Reading the Signs and other itinerant essays | Stephen Benz
Topographies | Stephen Benz
What We Ask of Flesh | Remica L. Bingham
The Greatest Jewish-American Lover in Hungarian History | Michael Blumenthal
No Hurry | Michael Blumenthal
Choir of the Wells | Bruce Bond
Cinder | Bruce Bond
The Other Sky | Bruce Bond and Aron Wiesenfeld
Peal | Bruce Bond
Scar | Bruce Bond
Until We Talk | Darrell Bourque and Bill Gingles
Poems and Their Making: A Conversation | Moderated by Philip Brady
Crave: Sojourn of a Hungry Soul | Laurie Jean Cannady
Toucans in the Arctic | Scott Coffel
Sixteen | Auguste Corteau
Wattle & daub | Brian Coughlan
Body of a Dancer | Renée E. D'Aoust
Generations: Lullaby with Incendiary Device, The Nazi Patrol, and How It Is That We | Dante Di Stefano, William Heyen, and H. L. Hix
Ill Angels | Dante Di Stefano
Aard-vark to Axolotl: Pictures From my Grandfather's Dictionary | Karen Donovan
Trio: Planet Parable, Run: A Verse-History of Victoria Woodhull, and Endless Body | Karen Donovan, Diane Raptosh, and Daneen Wardrop
Scything Grace | Sean Thomas Dougherty
Areas of Fog | Will Dowd
Romer | Robert Eastwood
Wait for God to Notice| Sari Fordham
Bon Courage: Essays on Inheritance, Citizenship, and a Creative Life | Ru Freeman
Surrendering Oz | Bonnie Friedman
Nahoonkara | Peter Grandbois
Triptych: The Three-Legged World, In Time, and Orpheus & Echo | Peter Grandbois, James McCorkle, and Robert Miltner
The Candle: Poems of Our 20th Century Holocausts | William Heyen
The Confessions of Doc Williams & Other Poems | William Heyen
The Football Corporations | William Heyen
A Poetics of Hiroshima | William Heyen
September 11, 2001: American Writers Respond | Edited by William Heyen
Shoah Train | William Heyen
American Anger: An Evidentiary | H. L. Hix
As Easy As Lying | H. L. Hix

As Much As, If Not More Than | H. L. Hix
Chromatic | H. L. Hix
Demonstrategy: Poetry, For and Against | H. L. Hix
First Fire, Then Birds | H. L. Hix
God Bless | H. L. Hix
I'm Here to Learn to Dream in Your Language | H. L. Hix
Incident Light | H. L. Hix
Legible Heavens | H. L. Hix
Lines of Inquiry | H. L. Hix
Rain Inscription | H. L. Hix
Shadows of Houses | H. L. Hix
Wild and Whirling Words: A Poetic Conversation | Moderated by H. L. Hix
All the Difference | Patricia Horvath
Art Into Life | Frederick R. Karl
Free Concert: New and Selected Poems | Milton Kessler
Who's Afraid of Helen of Troy: An Essay on Love | David Lazar
Black Metamorphoses | Shanta Lee
Mailer's Last Days: New and Selected Remembrances of a Life in Literature |
J. Michael Lennon
Parallel Lives | Michael Lind
The Burning House | Paul Lisicky
Museum of Stones | Lynn Lurie
Quick Kills | Lynn Lurie
Synergos | Roberto Manzano
The Gambler's Nephew | Jack Matthews
American Mother | Colum McCann with Diane Foley
The Subtle Bodies | James McCorkle
An Archaeology of Yearning | Bruce Mills
Arcadia Road: A Trilogy | Thorpe Moeckel
Venison | Thorpe Moeckel
So Late, So Soon | Carol Moldaw
The Widening | Carol Moldaw
Clay and Star: Selected Poems of Liliana Ursu | Translated by Mihaela Moscaliuc
Cannot Stay: Essays on Travel | Kevin Oderman
White Vespa | Kevin Oderman
Also Dark | Angelique Palmer
Fates: The Medea Notebooks, Starfish Wash-Up, and overflow of an unknown self |
Ann Pedone, Katherine Soniat, and D. M. Spitzer
The Dog Looks Happy Upside Down | Meg Pokrass
Mr. Either/Or | Aaron Poochigian
Mr. Either/Or : All the Rage | Aaron Poochigian
The Shyster's Daughter | Paula Priamos
Help Wanted: Female | Sara Pritchard
American Amnesiac | Diane Raptosh
Dear Z: The Zygote Epistles | Diane Raptosh
Human Directional | Diane Raptosh
50 Miles | Sheryl St. Germain
Saint Joe's Passion | J.D. Schraffenberger

Lies Will Take You Somewhere | Sheila Schwartz
Fast Animal | Tim Seibles
One Turn Around the Sun | Tim Seibles
Voodoo Libretto: New and Selected Poems | Tim Seibles
Rough Ground | Alix Anne Shaw
A Heaven Wrought of Iron: Poems From the Odyssey | D. M. Spitzer
American Fugue | Alexis Stamatis
Variations in the Key of K | Alex Stein
The Casanova Chronicles | Myrna Stone
Luz Bones | Myrna Stone
In the Cemetery of the Orange Trees | Jeff Talarigo
The White Horse: A Colombian Journey | Diane Thiel
The Arsonist's Song Has Nothing to Do With Fire | Allison Titus
Bestiality of the Involved | Spring Ulmer
Silk Road | Daneen Wardrop
Sinnerman | Michael Waters
The Fugitive Self | John Wheatcroft
YOU. | Joseph P. Wood

Etruscan Press Is Proud of Support Received From

Wilkes University

Wilkes University

Ohio Arts Council

The Stephen & Jeryl Oristaglio Foundation

Community of Literary Magazines and Presses

National Endowment for the Arts

Drs. Barbara Brothers & Gratia Murphy Endowment

Founded in 2001 with a generous grant from the Oristaglio Foundation, Etruscan Press is a nonprofit cooperative of poets and writers working to produce and promote books that nurture the dialogue among genres, achieve a distinctive voice, and reshape the literary and cultural histories of which we are a part.

Etruscan Press
www.etruscanpress.org
Etruscan Press books may be ordered from

Consortium Book Sales and Distribution
800.283.3572
www.cbsd.com

Etruscan Press is a 501(c)(3) nonprofit organization.
Contributions to Etruscan Press are tax deductible
as allowed under applicable law.

For more information, a prospectus,
or to order one of our titles,
contact us at books@etruscanpress.org.

Printed in the USA
CPSIA information can be obtained
at www.ICGtesting.com
JSHW080232280324
60018JS00001B/1

9 798985 882483